WHEREVER I LIE IS YOUR BED

WHEREVER I LIE IS YOUR BED

*Edited by Margaret Jull Costa
and Marilyn Hacker*

TWO LINES   WORLD WRITING IN TRANSLATION   XVI

FOUNDING EDITOR   *Olivia E. Sears*

POETRY EDITOR   *Marilyn Hacker*

PROSE EDITOR   *Margaret Jull Costa*

PUBLICATIONS MANAGER   *Annie Janusch*

PN
6010
.W52
2009

Endpaper: Ibrahim Nasrallah, "She Talks About Their Field"
("Fi hadithiha 'an haqlhima"), from *Bism al-'umm wa al-ibn*.
(Beirut: Al Mu'assasa al-'Arabiyya li aldirasat wa al-nashr,
1999), translated by Rasheeda Plenty.

Wherever I Lie Is Your Bed
TWO LINES World Writing in Translation
no. 16

ISBN 978-1-931883-16-0

Cover photos by Tag Savage and Annie Janusch
Book design by Tag Savage

Printed in Canada by Friesens Corporation

Distributed by The University of Washington Press

TWO LINES is indexed in the MLA International
Bibliography.

Contents

Focus on Palestinian Poetry | Edited by Marilyn Hacker

Endpaper

Editors' Notes

When I translate, which is most days, I am always trying to capture, reproduce, become the author's voice, and when I read translations, what I look for is a voice, one that I want to listen to, a voice that convinces in English. My selection of prose pieces for this volume of TWO LINES was guided by that desire to be convinced, and what I thought would be an impossible task was, it turned out, very easy. I just listened and chose those voices I most wanted to carry on hearing. And what was so exhilarating about hearing and reading these stories and extracts was not only the sheer variety of experience they encapsulate—from Emily Dickinson dying in Amherst to a rabbi trying to rediscover his identity in Brooklyn to Hamza leaving Sudan in search of work wherever he can find it—but also the sense of estrangement that fills so many of them. In *The Naked Eye*, a Vietnamese girl ends up in Paris not knowing a word of French; *Azorno* is full of shifting identities and locations; in "The Man Who Tried to Go to Heaven" a young boy is transplanted to a strange land and a still stranger situation. We have a French author writing about an American poet, a Japanese author writing in German about a Vietnamese girl adrift in Paris, a Cuban author (and translator of Russian literature) writing about Russians and diamonds and the mafia on the Costa del Sol. These stories throw open windows onto exhilarating and troubling worlds. And that is surely what translation aspires to do.

MARGARET JULL COSTA

A map crumpled like politics—
torn and sullied like the ethics of nation states.—

. . . writes Kurdish poet Sherko Bekes in Choman Hardi's translation. The map, for the poets in this volume, is sometimes the record of a diasporic and ongoing journey, even for those who are not, like Bekes's speaker, in some kind of exile. The youthful Berliners of Andrej Glusgold's and Chris Michalski's poems seem on the point of a Rimbaldian departure. There seems to be no abode but the beloved himself for the persona of the Hungarian Anna Szabo's *This Day*, and the shifting cityscapes make it clear that this is also a condition of the uncertainties around them. The supremely "vexed" question of a place that can accept them both at once, and which they can accept in turn, is central to the erotically charged struggle of the lovers in Mahmoud Darwish's *Rita's Winter*. And it is the Basque language being crumpled into erasure in Kirmen Uribe's witty poem which manages its own re-inscriptions. While I did not consciously seek poets inscribing (or refusing) new and invisible borders, a cohort similar to Breyten Breytenbach's *apatride* citizens of "Mor"—an invented word halfway between "love" and "death,"—many of the most initially gripping and subsequently memorable translations I encountered in making this difficult (because so limited) selection seemed to share that liminality. (Not the Haitian René Depestre, locating a household around the deity of a sewing machine—and not younger Palestinian poets Najwan Darwish and Ayman Ghbarieh, humorously and defiantly rooted.) All these poems, of origins and blurrings, now have new roots as poems in English, thanks to their translators' inspired and judicious gardening.

MARILYN HACKER

WHEREVER I LIE IS YOUR BED

Poems by Adonis

Translated by Khaled Mattawa from Arabic (Syria)

Adonis (Ali Ahmad Said Esber) was born in 1930 in the village of Qassabin in Syria. The Arab world's senior leading poet, he has produced some of the most innovative poetry in Arabic to draw on both classical Arabic literature and on avant-garde Western poetics. Among his more than two dozen books of poetry from six decades of writing, his best-known works are *Mihyar al-Dimashqi* (*Mihayar of Damascus*, BOA Editions), *Mufrad bi-sighat al-jam'* (Singular in the Plural Form), *Kitab al-hissar* (The Book of Siege), and the three-volume *Al-kitab* (The Book). Adonis has produced several seminal and highly controversial books of cultural criticism centered on poetics, *Al-thabit wal mutahawil* (The Constant and

the Changing) and *Al-shi'iriya al-arabiya* (Arab Poetics). Adonis's poetry has been translated into dozens of languages, and he has received numerous prestigious awards in the Arab world and Europe, most recently the 'Uweiss Prize (UAE) in 2005 and the Bjørnson Prize (Norway) in 2007.

The short poems in this selection are from the book *Al-mutabaqat wal-al-awaiil* (Similarities and Beginnings) published in Beirut in 1980. Adonis had devoted the 1970s to the long poem form. By the time he published *Al-mutabaqat*, he had written his "Hada huwa ismi" (This is My Name) and "Qabr li New York" (A Grave for New York), two remarkable, and very different, medium-length

3

poems of startling originality and philosophical depth that established him as the most innovative poet in the Arabic language. These two poems are probably Adonis's most extroverted, addressing such issues as Arab identity and global capitalism, though with great subtlety. In 1977 he published a 400-page book-length poem, *Mufrad bi-sighat al-jam'* (Singular in the Plural Form), the most complex of his works up to then, a dazzling and talismanic meditation on the body and the mysteries of eros.

The "Beginnings" presented here are therefore a sort of reaction to the long poem and a retreat to Adonis's earlier practice of writing the *qit'a* (short piece) poem. In the early 1960s, Adonis had adopted the short poem, generally without rhyme and with a loose meter, as a response to the lyrical verbosity that characterized Arab poetry at the time. Adonis's short poems then did not engage contemporary politics, focusing instead on existential meditation in the hope of generating new abstract and conceptual paradigms in the Arab arts. This was not art for art's sake, as he and his colleagues at *Shi'ir* magazine, contended. Rather, what the Arab and Islamic world needed then, according to Adonis, was a poetry that expanded the reader's imaginative horizons and promoted a true freedom which is born in the mind and the spirit before it takes on concrete reality.

In these short poems written in the early 1980s, a sense of a larger project seems to have guided his process. The book in which they appeared contains twenty-eight poems in its "Similarities" section, which address varied subjects, such as the poet's village, a city square, and the poet's favorite poets. The "Beginnings" section includes thirty-eight poems focused on stages of life and states of mind. Adonis here creates a divide between memory and consciousness, biography and philosophy, similar perhaps to Blake's division between innocence and experience (a work that Adonis may have read in French). One can perhaps read *Al-mutabaqat wal-al-awaiil* (Similarities and Beginnings) as one long two-part poem. But the thrill of these poems is the crystalline focus that Adonis brings to each subject he addresses, demonstrating that his lyric touch is as powerful as his epic sweep.

Original text: Adonis, *Al-mutabaqat wal-al-awaiil.*
Beirut: Dar al-awdah, 1980.

أول الظن

ها أنا أولدُ الآنَ—
أرنو إلى الناس:
أعشق هذا الأنينَ / الفضاءْ
أعشق هذا الغبار يغطي الجبينَ / تتوّرتُ
أرنو إلى الناس – نبعٌ / شَرَرْ
أتقرّى رسوميَ – لا شكلَ غيرُ الحنين
وهذا البهاءْ
في غُبار البشَرْ.

The Beginning of Doubt

Here I am being born—
seeking people.
I love this sighing, this space.
I love this dust that covers brows. I am illuminated.
I seek people—a spring and sparks.
I read my drawings—nothing but longing—
and this glory
in people's dust.

أول الكتاب

فاعلاً, أو ضميراً ـ
والزمانُ هو الوصفُ. ماذا؟ تكلمتَ, أو يتكلم
باسمكَ شيءٌ؟

...

تستعيرُ؟ المجازُ غطاءٌ
والغطاء هو التَّيْهُ ـ
هذي حياتُكَ تجتاحها كلماتٌ
لا تُقرّ المعاجمُ أسرارَها / كلماتٌ
لا تجيبُ, ولكنها تتساءلُ ـ تِيةٌ
والمجازُ انتقالٌ
بين نار ونارٍ
بين موت وموتٍ.

...

أنتَ هذا العبور الذي يتقرى, ويولد في كل معنى:
لن يكون لوجهكَ وصفٌ.

The Beginning of Inscription

A subject or a pronoun—
and time is the adjective. What? Did you speak, or is something
        speaking in your name?

What to borrow? Metaphor is a cover
and a cover is loss.
Here is your life being invaded by words.
Dictionaries do not give away their secrets and words
do not answer, they go on questioning—loss
and metaphor in transition
from one fire to another
one death to another.

You are this passage being deciphered, born in each interpretation:
There will be no way to describe your face.

أول العشق

قرأ العاشقون الجراحَ / كتبنا الجراحْ
زمناً آخراً, ورسمْنا
وقتنا:
وجهيَ المساءُ, وأهدابك الصباحْ
وخُطانا دمٌ وحنينٌ
مثلهم /
كلما استيقظوا, قطفونا
ورَمَوْا حبّهم ورمونا
وَرْدَةً للرياحْ.

The Beginning of Love

Lovers read their wounds, and we wrote them
     as another era, then drew
     our time:
     My face is evening, your eye lashes are dawn.
Our steps are blood and longing
     like theirs.

Every time they woke, they plucked us
and tossed their love away and tossed us,
a flower in the wind.

أول الطريق

الليلُ كانَ وَرَقاً – وكنّا
حبراً:
– "رسمتَ وجهاً, أو حجراً؟"
– " رسمتِ وجهاً أو حجراً؟ "
ولم أُجِبْ,
ولم تُجِبْ / عشقنا
سكوتَنا, – ليست له طريقٌ
كحبّنا – ليست له طريقٌ...

The Beginning of the Road

Night was paper, and we were
    ink:
—"Did you draw a face, or a stone?"
—"Did you draw a face, or a stone?"
I did not answer
nor did she. Our love,
our silence—has no inroads
our love—no roads lead to it.

أول الاسم

أيامي اسمُها
والحلمُ, حين تسهرُ السماء في أحزاني, اسمُها
والهاجسُ اسمُها
والعُرْسُ, حين يُمزَجُ الذابح بالذبيحةِ, اسمُها
...
ومرةً غنّيتُ: كل وردةٍ
في التعبِ, اسمُها
في السفرِ, اسمُها
...
هل انتهى الطريقُ, هل تغيّر اسمُها؟

The Beginning of the Name

My days are her name
and the dream, when the sky spends her night inside my sadness, are her name.
Premonition is her name
and the feast, when the slaughterer and the slaughtered are one, are her name.

Once I sang: every rose
in fatigue, is her name
in travel, her name.

Has the road come to an end? Has she changed her name?

The Tin Drum

Günter Grass | Translated by Breon Mitchell from German (Germany)

On a warm summer day in 2005, the citizens of Gdańsk, Poland, were treated to an unusual sight: one of their favorite sons, Günter Grass, had returned, and he appeared to be conducting a tour. As he pointed out the special features of historical buildings in the Altstadt, the dozen or so men and women gathered around him seemed to be paying unusually close attention. And well they might, for each was hard at work retranslating Grass's most famous novel, set in Danzig, into his or her respective language, in celebration of the fiftieth anniversary of its original publication.

For over a week, the Nobel Prize-winning author had been conferring with his translators, going over *Die Blechtrommel* page by page, then emerging from the workshop atmosphere to show them the heart and soul of the novel's geography and history—the potato fields of the Kashubian countryside, the beach and jetty at Neufahrwasser, the city and suburbs of Danzig, Oskar's home, the grocery store, the old city hall: in short, the still living features of his past.

We were free to ask any question we wished, and Grass always answered directly and clearly, with unfailing good humor. In more than 2,500 instances, carefully noted page by page in a protocol each translator later received, he clarified the meaning of a word or phrase, noting a particular linguistic effect, urging us to capture a special nuance.

He called our attention to his own idiosyncratic style —his penchant, for example, for writing numbers and dates out in full, rather than using Arabic numerals. He requested that we indulge him in this, pointing out that this practice struck German publishers as strange, too. He asked us to follow Oskar's odd predilection for the use of the superlative, a verbal tic seldom noted in previous versions. He asked that we differentiate the characters more carefully in spoken dialogue, particularly with regard to variations in dialect, grammatical usage, and vocabulary.

He was anything but dictatorial, however. In passages involving complicated wordplay, or strongly marked by rhythm, he told us just to do our best, trusting us to come up with similar effects in our own languages, and encouraging us to coin new words where he had invented new ones in German. And on almost every page, he read one or more passages aloud, stressing the musicality of the language. Over the course of those days in Gdańsk, nothing made a more lasting impression on us than the sound of his voice, the melody of the text, the rhythm of Oskar's drum.

The challenge of *The Tin Drum* has been remarkable. But nothing can match the challenge it must have posed almost fifty years ago. I am only too aware of the shortcomings of my own translation and of the debt I owe to Ralph Manheim, whose beautiful version helped ensure the novel's original success. It is my own good fortune to have shared some part of this long journey with him.

Original text: Günter Grass,
Die Blechtrommel. Munich: Luchterhand, 1959.

Die Blechtrommel

Der weite Rock

Meine Großmutter Anna Bronski saß an einem späten Oktobernachmittag in ihren Röcken am Rande eines Kartoffelackers. Am Vormittag hätte man sehen können, wie es die Großmutter verstand, das schlaffe Kraut zu ordentlichen Haufen zu rechen, mittags aß sie ein mit Sirup versüßtes Schmalzbrot, hackte dann letztmals den Acker nach, saß endlich in ihren Röcken zwischen zwei fast vollen Körben. Vor senkrecht gestellten, mit den Spitzen zusammenstrebenden Stiefelsohlen schwelte ein manchmal asthmatisch auflebendes, den Rauch flach und umständlich über die kaum geneigte Erdkruste hinschickendes Kartoffelkrautfeuer. Man schrieb das Jahr neunundneunzig, sie saß im Herzen der Kaschubei, nahe bei Bissau, noch näher der Ziegelei, vor Ramkau saß sie, hinter Viereck, in Richtung der Straße nach Brentau, zwischen Dirschau und Karthaus, den schwarzen Wald Goldkrug in Rücken saß sie und schob mit einem an der Spitze verkohlten Haselstock Kartoffeln unter die heiße Asche.

Wenn ich soeben den Rock meiner Großmutter besonders erwähnte, hoffentlich deutlich genug sagte: Sie saß in ihren Röcken—ja, das Kapitel "Der weite Rock" überschreibe, weiß ich, was ich diesem Kleidungsstück schuldig bin. Meine Großmutter trug nicht nur einen Rock, vier Röcke trug sie übereinander. Nicht etwa, daß sie einen Ober- und drei Unterröcke getragen hätte; vier sogenannte Oberröcke trug sie, ein Rock trug den nächsten, sie aber trug alle vier nach einem System, das die Reihenfolge der Röcke von Tag zu Tag veränderte. Was gestern oben saß, saß heute gleich darunter; der zweite war der dritte Rock. Was gestern noch dritter Rock war, war ihr heute der Haut nahe. . . .

The Tin Drum

The Wide Skirt

My grandmother Anna Bronski sat in her skirts late one October afternoon at the edge of a potato field. You could have seen how expertly my grandmother raked the limp potato tops into tidy piles that morning, ate a hunk of bread at noon smeared with dripping and sweetened with syrup, dug through the field one last time, and sat at last in her skirts between two nearly full baskets. Before the upturned and inwardly tilted soles of her boots, flaring up asthmatically from time to time and sending a flat layer of troubled smoke across the slightly tilted crust of the soil, smoldered a potato-top fire. The year was eighteen ninety-nine, she sat in the heart of Kashubia, near Bissau, nearer still to the brickworks, this side of Ramkau she sat, beyond Viereck, facing the road to Brentau, between Dirschau and Karthaus, with her back toward the black forest of Goldkrug she sat, shoving potatoes under the hot ashes with the charred tip of a hazel stick.

If I've singled out my grandmother's skirt for special mention, making it clear, I hope, that she was sitting in her skirts—even calling the chapter "The Wide Skirt"—it's because I know how much I owe to that article of clothing. My grandmother didn't wear just one skirt, she wore four, one atop the other. Nor did she wear one top skirt and three underskirts; she wore four so-called top skirts, each skirt wore another, but she wore all four, according to a system of daily rotation. The skirt on top the day before descended one layer on the next, her second skirt became the third. The skirt that yesterday was third now nestled right against her skin. Yesterday's inmost skirt now clearly showed its pattern, which was none at all: my grandmother Anna Bronski's skirts all preferred the same standard potato color. It must have suited her.

Aside from their color my grandmother's skirts were distinguished by a lavish expanse of material. They formed broad arcs, billowed when the wind rose, fell slack when it had had enough, rattled as it passed, and all four flew out ahead of her when the wind was in her stern. When she sat down, my grandmother gathered her skirts about her.

In addition to the four skirts that permanently billowed, drooped, draped, or stood stiff and empty by her bed, my grandmother possessed a fifth. This skirt differed in no way from the four other potato-colored ones. And this fifth skirt was not always the same fifth skirt. Like its brothers—for skirts are masculine by nature—it too was subject to rotation, was one of the four skirts she wore, and like them, when its time had come each fifth Friday, it descended into the washtub, hung Saturday on the clothesline at the kitchen window, and lay when dry on the ironing board.

When, after one of these housecleaning-baking-washing-and-ironing Saturdays, having milked and fed the cow, my grandmother climbed into the tub, tendered something to the suds, let the tub water sink once more, then sat in her grandly flowered towel on the edge of the bed, there were four skirts and the freshly washed one lying spread out before her on the floor. She propped up the lower lid of her right eye with her right forefinger, consulted no one, not even her brother Vinzent, and thus reached a speedy conclusion. Barefoot she stood and pushed aside with her toe the skirt whose potato sheen had lost the most luster. The clean one then took its place.

The following Sunday, to the greater glory of Jesus, about whom she had firm ideas, she would consecrate the new order of skirts by attending church in Ramkau. Where did my grandmother wear the freshly laundered skirt? Not only a clean woman but also somewhat vain, she wore the best one on top, and if the weather was good, in bright sunshine.

Now it was a Monday afternoon and my grandmother was sitting by the potato fire. Her Sunday skirt had moved one closer to her Monday, while the one skin-warmed on Sunday flowed atop her hips that Monday Monday-dull. She whistled, with no particular tune in mind, and scraped the first baked potato from the ashes with her hazel stick. She shoved the spud far enough from the smoldering mound of tops for the breeze to caress and cool it. A sharpened stick then speared the split, charred, and crusty tuber and held it to her mouth, which no longer whistled but instead, through cracked and wind-dried lips, blew ashes and earth from the skin.

As she blew, my grandmother closed her eyes. When she thought she had blown long enough, she opened her eyes, one after the other, bit down with her peep-through but otherwise perfect front teeth, quickly released them, held the still too hot potato half, mealy and steaming, in her open mouth, and inhaling smoke and October air, stared with rounded eyes over her flaring nostrils across the field to the nearby horizon with its grid of telegraph poles and the top third of the brickworks chimney.

Something was moving between the telegraph poles. My grandmother closed her mouth, sucked in her lips, narrowed her eyes, and munched on the potato. Something was moving between the telegraph poles. Something was leaping. Three men were leaping between the poles, three made for the chimney, then round in front, when one of them doubled back, took a new running start, seemed short and stout, made it over the chimney, over the brickworks, the other two, more tall and thin, made it over the brickworks too, if only just, between the poles again, but short and stout doubled back and short and stout was in a greater hurry than tall and thin, the other leapers, who had to head back toward the chimney because the other man was already tumbling over it, while the two, still hot on his heels, made a running start and were suddenly gone, had lost heart it seemed, and the short one too fell in midleap from the chimney and disappeared below the horizon.

And there they stayed, it was intermission, or they were changing costumes, or coating bricks and getting paid for it.

When my grandmother tried to take advantage of the intermission to spear a second potato, she missed it.

For the one who seemed short and stout now climbed, in the same costume, over the horizon as if it were a picket fence, as if he'd left the two leapers who were chasing him behind the fence, among the bricks, or on the pike to Brentau, yet was still in a great hurry, trying to outrace the telegraph poles, taking long, slow leaps across the field, mud leaping from his soles as he leapt from the mud, but no matter how far he leapt, he merely crept, he crawled across the muddy earth. At times he seemed stuck to the ground, then hung suspended in air so long that short and stout he still had time to wipe his brow in midleap before planting his leg again in the freshly plowed field that furrowed toward the sunken lane by her five-acre field of potatoes.

And he made it to the sunken lane, had barely vanished short and stout into the sunken lane, when tall and thin the other two, who may have toured the brickworks meanwhile, climbed likewise over the horizon and stomped their way tall and thin but by no means slim across the field, so that my grandmother failed once more to spear her potato; because that's a sight you don't see every day, three grown men, albeit grown in quite different ways, hopping among telegraph poles, practically breaking off the brickworks chimney, then, at intervals, first short and stout, then thin and tall, but all three struggling hard, ever more mud clinging to their freshly polished boots, leaping through the field that Vinzent had plowed just two days before, and disappearing into the sunken lane.

Now all three were gone, and my grandmother dared spear a nearly cold potato. Hastily she blew earth and ashes from the skin, put the whole thing in her mouth at once, thinking, if she was thinking, that they must be from the brickworks, and was still chewing with a circular motion when one of them leapt out of the sunken lane, glanced about wildly over his black mustache, took two final leaps to the fire, stood on this, that, and the other side of the fire all at once, fled here, was scared there, didn't know where to head, couldn't go back, since tall and thin were coming up the sunken lane behind him, clapped his hands, slapped his knees, his eyes popping from his head, sweat leaping from his brow. And panting, mustache trembling, he ventured nearer, crept right up to the soles of her boots; crept right up to my grandmother, looked at my grandmother like some short, stout animal, at which she heaved a great sigh, stopped chewing her potato, tilted apart the soles of her boots, abandoned all thought of brickworks, bricks, brick makers and brick coaters, and instead lifted her skirt, no, lifted all four of them, all up at once, so that this man who was not from the brickworks could crawl short but stout beneath them, and then he was gone with his mustache, gone with his animal look, came neither from Ramkau nor Viereck, was under her skirts with his fear, his knee-slapping ended, not stout or short, yet still taking up space, panting and trembling and hands on knees now forgotten: all was as still as on the first day of Creation or the last, a slight breeze gossiped in the potato fire, the telegraph poles counted themselves in silence, the brickworks chimney stood firm, and she, my grandmother, she smoothed her top skirt over the second skirt, smooth and proper, scarcely felt him under the fourth skirt, had not yet caught on with her third to something new and amazing against her skin. And because it was amazing, though on top all was calm, and both second and third had yet to catch on, she scraped two or three potatoes from the ashes, took four raw ones from the basket by her right elbow, shoved the raw spuds into the hot ashes one by one, covered them with more ashes, and poked about until the thick smoke billowed up once more—what else could she have done?

My grandmother's skirts had barely settled down, the thick flow of smoke from the potato fire, which had lost its way during all the desperate knee-slapping, place-changing, and poking about, had barely returned to creep yellow windward across the field to the southwest, when the tall and thin pair chasing the short but stout fellow now living under her skirts spurted forth from the lane and turned out to be tall and thin and wearing the official uniform of the rural constabulary.

They almost shot past my grandmother. Didn't one of them even leap over the fire? But suddenly they had heels, and brains in their heels, dug them in, turned, stomped back, stood booted and uniformed in the thick smoke, withdrew coughing in their uniforms, pulling smoke along, and were still coughing as they addressed my grandmother, wanting to know if she'd seen Koljaiczek, she must have seen him, she was sitting by the lane and he, Koljaiczek, had escaped along the lane.

My grandmother hadn't seen any Koljaiczek, because she didn't know any Koljaiczek. Was he from the brickworks, she asked, because the only ones she knew were from the brickworks. But this Koljaiczek the uniforms described had nothing to do with bricks, he was more on the short and stout side. My grandmother thought back, recalled having seen someone like that run past, and pointed, with reference to where he was heading, with a steaming potato spitted on a sharpened stick in the direction of Bissau, which, to judge by the potato, must lie between the sixth and seventh telegraph poles, counting to the right from the chimney of the brickworks. But my grandmother had no idea if the man running was Koljaiczek, blamed her lack of knowledge on the fire at the soles of her boots; it gave her enough to do, it was burning poorly, she didn't have time to worry about people running past or standing in the smoke, in general she didn't worry about people she didn't know, the only ones she knew were from Bissau, Ramkau, Viereck, and the brickworks—and that was plenty for her.

Having said this, my grandmother heaved a gentle sigh, but loud enough that the uniforms asked why she was sighing. She nodded toward the fire to indicate that she was sighing because the little fire was burning poorly, and because of all the people standing right in the smoke, then she bit off half the potato with her widely spaced front teeth, lost herself entirely in chewing, and rolled her eyeballs up and to the left.

The men in the uniform of the rural constabulary could draw no encouragement from the distant gaze of my grandmother, nor were they sure if they should head off beyond the telegraph poles toward Bissau, so in the meantime they poked around with their bayonets in the nearby piles of potato tops not yet burning. Moved by a sudden inspiration, they simultaneously overturned both nearly full potato baskets at my grandmother's elbows, and couldn't understand why only potatoes rolled out of the woven baskets at their boots, and not Koljaiczek. Suspiciously they crept around the potato pile, as if Koljaiczek might somehow have had time to pile into it, gave it several well-aimed jabs, and were sorry when no one screamed. Their suspicions were aroused by every bush, however scraggly, every mouse hole, a colony of molehills, and time and again by my grandmother, who sat there as if rooted, emitting sighs, rolling her eyes behind her lids so that the whites showed, reciting the Kashubian names of all the saints—all of which expressed and emphasized the sorrows of a poorly burning little fire and two overturned potato baskets.

The uniforms stayed a good half-hour. They stood at varying distances from the fire, took bearings on the brickworks chimney, intending to occupy Bissau as well, postponed the attack, and held their reddish blue hands over the fire till my grandmother, without ever interrupting her sighs, gave each of them a split potato on a stick. But in the midst of their chewing, the uniforms remembered their uniforms, leapt a stone's throw into the field along the broom at the edge of the lane, and startled a hare

that did not, however, turn out to be Koljaiczek. Back at the fire they recovered their mealy, hotly aromatic spuds, and pacified as well as somewhat war-weary, decided to gather up the raw spuds and return them to the baskets they had overturned earlier in the line of duty.

Only when evening began to squeeze a fine, slanting rain and an inky twilight from the October sky did they attack, briefly and listlessly, a distant, darkening boulder, but once that was taken care of they decided to call it a day. A bit more foot-stamping and hands held out in blessing over the rain-spattered little fire, its thick smoke spreading, more coughing in the green smoke, eyes tearing up in the yellow smoke, then a coughing, teary-eyed stomping toward Bissau. If Koljaiczek wasn't here, then Koljaiczek must be in Bissau. The rural constabulary never sees more than two possibilities.

The smoke from the slowly dying fire enveloped my grandmother like a fifth skirt, so roomy that she too, in her four skirts, with her sighs and names of saints, like Koljaiczek, found herself beneath a skirt. Only when nothing remained of the uniforms but wavering dots slowly drowning in dusk between the telegraph poles did my grandmother rise as laboriously as if she had struck root and was now interrupting that incipient growth, pulling forth tendrils and earth.

Suddenly finding himself lying short and stout in the rain without a hood, Koljaiczek grew cold. Quickly he buttoned the trousers that fear and an overwhelming need for refuge had bidden him open under her skirts. He fiddled quickly with the buttons, fearing an all too rapid cooling of his rod, for the weather carried the threat of autumnal chills.

It was my grandmother who found four more hot potatoes under the ashes. She gave three to Koljaiczek, kept one for herself, then asked before taking a bite if he came from the brickworks, though she must have known that Koljaiczek had nothing to do with the bricks. And paying no heed to his answer, she loaded the lighter basket onto him, bent beneath the heavier one herself, kept one hand free for the garden rake and hoe, and with basket, potatoes, rake, and hoe, billowed away in her four skirts toward Bissau-Abbau.

Bissau-Abbau was not Bissau proper. It lay more in the direction of Ramkau. Leaving the brickworks to their left, they headed for the black forest, where Goldkrug lay, and beyond it Brentau. But in a hollow before the forest lay Bissau-Abbau. And following my grandmother toward it short and stout came Joseph Koljaiczek, who could no longer free himself from her skirts.

Poems by Mikhail Yeryomin

Translated by J. Kates from Russian (Russia)

Mikhail Fyodorovich Yeryomin was born in 1936 in the northern Caucasus but grew up in Leningrad, where he studied in the Philology Department of the Leningrad State University and graduated from the Herzen Institute. A close friend and associate of Joseph Brodsky's before his exile, Yeryomin is a playwright and a translator (of T.S. Eliot, Hart Crane, W.B. Yeats, M. Ikbal, and Khushkhal-khan Khattak, among others) who saw few of his poems published in his homeland during the Soviet period. Instead, his work appeared in émigré journals like *Kontinent* and *Ekho*. The first volume of his poems to appear in Russian was published in the United States in 1986, but not until 1991 in Moscow. Each new book is a cumulative edition to, and a selection from, his previous work, and each carries the same title: *Stikhotvorenia* (Poems). So far, there have been six of these (1986, 1991, 1996, 1998, 2002, and 2005). Yeryomin currently lives in St. Petersburg.

Yeryomin has been writing his characteristic eight-line stanzas for more than half a century, adding slowly to a body of work that is unique in Russian poetry and that may be compared only, perhaps, to Ezra Pound's *Cantos* or John Berryman's *Dream Songs* in English. Yeryomin draws on a wide range of languages—including real and made-up hieroglyphics, classical quotations, and scientific and technical vocabularies and formulae—to compose these tight constructions. Over the years, the emphases of sound patterns and languages have changed, but the body of work exists as a unity. The poems included here represent a sampling across the decades.

The poet and I have worked together in forging these translations. Yeryomin is himself an accomplished translator from English but with his own idiosyncratic ideas. He occasionally insists on properties that force a translator to diverge from the literal into interpretation—and sometimes compel his collaborator to bite back. For instance, at one point the poet asked for a first line to consist of five unaccented syllables (paeans) in a row—a linguistic possibility in Russian but not in English. Faced with this, it was the poet who backed off. Whenever possible, of course, I have tried to accommodate his demands.

Yeryomin exploits more attributes of Russian than simply its stresses. His poems (especially the more recent ones) make use of infinitives and the particular Russian ability to communicate a whole clause in a single participle. Inevitably, English unpacks these.

Nevertheless, I hope I have been able to convey some of the rhythms, sound patterns, pyrotechnics, and terse economy of the originals.

Original text: Mikhail Yeryomin, *Stikhotvorenia, Ermitzah*. Tenafly, New Jersey: Hermitage, 1996; and Moscow: Pushkinsky Fond, 1998–2005.

Строител первого в мире моста
К месту строительства бревна таскал и доски,
Ладил настил, а потом настал
Час первой повозки.
Плотник локти положил на перила,
Трубкой украсил довольное лицо,
Выплеснул на рубаху бороды белила,
И стало мостостроение ремеслом отцов.

1958

The builder of the first bridge in the world
Dragged beams and boards to the construction site,
Steadied the planking, and then readied
The hour of the first vehicle.
The laborer laid his elbows on the railing,
His contented face reddened like a chimney,
He splashed whitewash onto the shirt of his beard
And began building bridges with his fathers' craft.

Терлось тельце телка
Об устойчивые стены стойла.
Нос коровий тельца толкал
Выводил на пустырь просторный.
Теленок вышел из коровника,
Стадности не стыдясь, пересек пустырь
И нежился в поле перстым курортником,
Жил, пережевывая стебли и лепестки.

1958

The heifer humped up against the calf
Around the stable walls of the stall.
The cow's nose shoved the calf,
Pushed it out into the open lot.
The calf came out of the cow-barn,
Without embarrassing the assembly, crossed the lot
And basked in the field like a motley sunbather,
Lived, surviving the stems and petals.

Животные обуваются в снежные следы
Или впадают в логово.
Растения гонимы холодом
В лабиринты корней и луковиц.
Люди уменшают до размером обуви
Присущие водоемам ладьи.
Подо льдом, как под теплым небом,
Фотолуг, фотолес, Фотолето.

1962

Animals put on shoes in snowy tracks
Or go to ground.
Plants persecuted by the cold
Fall into labyrinths of roots and bulbs.
People shrink as small as shoes
Like small boats on reservoirs.
Under the ice, as under a warm sky,
Photomeadow, photowood, photosummer.

$a^3 + y^3$ - заху есть ничто.

Ствол не насос, а высохший колодец.

Изоамиламина генератор

Жует подземные лучи.

Нелетний свет слепит растения.

Кольчуга склеренхимы холодна.

Засвечены фотоладони клёнов.

Горит осины санбенито.

1966–68

$a^3 + y^3$ - заху is nothingness.

A tree-trunk is not a pump, but a dry well.

A generator of isoamilamin

Munches on underground rays.

An unsummery light dazzles the plants.

The mail-shirt of sklerenchemistry is cold.

The photopalms of maples are overexposed.

Sanbenito of the aspens is on fire.

Rex

José Manuel Prieto | Translated by Esther Allen from Spanish (Cuba)

Rex is a novel about commentary, which is to say, about reading itself; it is therefore, I came to realize as I translated it, about translation, as well. Its protagonist-narrator is a tutor in the grotesquely luxurious home of a Russian family that is hiding out on Spain's Costa Brava some years after the collapse of the Soviet Union. The narrator, who is just as unreliable as everything else in sight here, loathes commentary above all things, and sees translation and the learning of foreign languages as entirely irrelevant. For him, there is only one Writer and only one Book, the source of all knowledge and the sole basis for the education he gives to Petya, his young charge: Proust's *A la recherche du temps perdu*. "What sense in learning a foreign language if, once within that other world or universe, you'd only be fatally drawn in again by the magnet of the Book? Better to focus on it, for it's the same in all languages, impervious—as the Commentator perversely affirms, though of course without referring directly to the Book—to the fire of translations."

Rex takes the form of a series of commentaries made to Petya by his tutor. These utterances are inchoate and mysterious, half-formed sentences often spoken at a fever pitch of emotion, without much in the way of context to help the reader determine when there's a shift between actual and hypothetical or imagined situations, between ranges of possible outcomes and the one we are to believe took place. Furthermore, the voice that speaks to us here is continually alluding to and citing from—in most unscholarly fashion—the entire gamut of world literature (all of which he attributes to the Writer), a wide array of scientific theories, and the history of Europe, particular the centuries of vicissitudes undergone by the Royal House of Russia. This last tendency drove the copy editor of the English translation to fill the margins of the galleys with commentaries of his own in the form of stern and increasingly irritated corrections: the narrator of *La recherche* does not give Albertine an airplane so that she can fly across Africa, we were admonished; Bach's Goldberg Variations were not first performed in Dresden, in 1947, for the benefit of the Russian ambassador; Jorge Luis Borges (a.k.a. the Commentator) and Marcel Proust never went on a long car trip together.

José Manuel Prieto grew up in Havana, then won a scholarship to study engineering at the University of Novosibirsk, the capital of Siberia. During the long period of his residence in Russia, the Soviet Union collapsed. He began his literary career as a translator from Russian to Spanish, and in this particular novel, even more so than in his two earlier ones, he writes as a translator, to expose the way in which all meaning is temporary and provisional, dependent upon its immediate context, subject to infinite and unpredictable shifts. Language, and the literary texts that are made from it, is not a diamond, its superhard molecules permanently ordered in a fixed pattern, its great value impervious to the ups and downs of the marketplace; it is, rather, a "luminous uproar," inevitably illusory and impermanent, dissolving into an ungraspably fine floating powder when any determined will is brought to bear on it. The English translation of *Rex* makes that point in a way its author, who finished writing the novel in 2006, could hardly have dreamed of. Though the book was written to describe "the strategies used to overcome the terrible experience of totalitarianism," as Prieto says in the Author's Note, the reader who comes to the English translation in 2009 won't be able to help reading this book, with its depiction of an obscene and ostentatious wealth founded on fakery, supposedly valuable objects that turn out to be of no value whatsoever, as being about a collapse much closer to home than that of the Soviet Union.

Though *Rex* is undoubtedly enriched by the added dimension that the current global economic crisis has bestowed upon it, its translation into other languages, other contexts, is only a first step on the way to what the text finally demands—translation into other mediums altogether. As I translated *Rex*, I kept visualizing it all on a stage, the protagonist a small figure at exact center, clutching his head in his hands, shouting and gesticulating as an endless kaleidoscope of vivid, projected images fill the air around him, and music plays. The best commentary that I can offer to the reader of *Rex* is the suggestion that it is less a novel than an opera; it should be read as an opera, and will, I hope, someday be performed as one.

Original Text: José Manuel Prieto, *Rex*.
Barcelona: Anagrama, 2007.

Rex

Tercer comentario

2

¿O cómo pensar en Nelly cómo en una gran dama? ¿Verla con los ojos con que el escritor, en el tercer libro, ve a su vecina. ¿Una gran dama como la princesa de Laumes? Y sí, inclinado por momentos a creerle. A pesar de la vulgaridad de la casa, de la turbiedad que imaginé en ella y que los insufribles muebles me inducían a pensar. Una mujer sobre la que podía colocar la elegancia natural de los Guermantes. Donde el escritor dice: **bajo una capota malva** un día, bajo una **toca azul marino** a la mañana siguiente. Y en todo este pasaje: **Una de las mañanas de cuaresma . . . me la encontré con un traje de terciopelo rojo claro, ligeramente escotado en el cuello.**

Sola, su marido vuelto a ir.

La manera con que dejaba clavada la mirada, en el mantel, inclinada la vista o cayendo en ángulo como un haz de luz. Y en el interior de aquel haz las figuritas de falsos antepasados ricos que jamás había tenido. Obsesionada con la idea de que habían sido nobles en algún punto, había Vasily Guennadovich, (tu papá) crecido en una familia de nobles, expropiados, esquilmados y escarnecidos por el año 17 y por los años 18 y 19 y 20. Robadas las fábricas que—mentía—, habían tenido en Finlandia. Al punto que le dije la primera vez en la cocina: deberías escribir, viajar a Tampere, buscar esos papeles.

Y se sonrió y me miró dos veces.

Yo habiendo sido buscado o contratado, terminé por entender, como una pieza más de aquél engaño, que les permitiría decir: "un preceptor para Petia, como lo tuvo Guennadi Nicolaevich, el abuelo de Vasily. Con una preparación, ¿sabes?. . .

Rex

Third Commentary

2

Now, how to think of Nelly as a great lady? To see her through the Writer's eyes when, in the third volume, he gazes at his neighbor. A great lady like the Princesse de Laumes? Yes, I was sometimes inclined to believe that. Despite the vulgarity of the house, the shady business I imagined going on there, which the unbearable furniture hinted at. A woman on whom I could confer all the natural elegance of the Guermantes. Where the Writer says: **beneath a mauve hood** one day, **a navy blue toque** the next morning. **And throughout this passage: One morning during Lent . . . I met her wearing a dress of pale red velvet, cut quite low at the neckline.**

Alone, her husband away again.

The way she would focus her gaze fixedly on the tablecloth, her eyes inclined or falling at an angle like a shaft of light. And in the interior of that shaft the tiny figures of the false rich ancestors she never had. Obsessed with the idea that they'd been aristocrats at some point, that Vasily Guennadovich (your father) had grown up in a family of nobles, dispossessed, stripped of everything and excoriated around the year '17 and through the years '18, '19, and '20. The factories they'd owned in Finland—she was lying—all stolen. To the point that I told her, that first time in the kitchen: You should write a letter, go to Tampere, find those papers.

And she smiled to herself and gave me two quick glances.

Having sought out and hired me, I finally understood, as one more element of that deception, which would permit them to say: "A tutor for Petya, just like the one Guennadi Nicolaevich, Vasily's grandfather, had. A certain level of instruction—you know?—a knowledge the boy would never have had access to in one of those schools, those prisons or warehouses for children, really. Although the one we hired is crazy or has had his brains scrambled by a writer he never stops talking about"—and she looked at me smiling when she thought that—"but he is good and generous and we have trusted him from the first moment."

With that facility for the third person so natural in intelligent women, which she used to downplay her obsession with the subject of nobility, speaking of herself as a more ironic, more observant person would, acting like a girl on a visit to someone else's house.

"She is, I confess, obsessed with the matter of nobility. And sometimes she'd like to fly away, escape from here. She'd love to pay you handsomely, to thank you for all that you do for her son . . . You don't wear rings?"

"I'd like to, you know?" I lowered my head toward her hand. Admirable, that blue gem, set high over the finger like a hard flower of stone.

I said nothing about her necklace, pretended she wasn't wearing the most fabulous necklace I'd seen in my life. Without taking my eyes off it, powerfully attracted by that necklace, fascinated and held by it, leaning toward her throat, with my feet firmly on the floor, imbibing the light her necklace radiated. Incredibly beautiful there on her breast. Obsessed with that necklace to the point that I'd searched through the fashion magazines they had lying around the house as instruction manuals for life in the West, scrutinizing the jeweled breast of every fashion model, Spanish or Greek, burnished skin glistening over the clavicle, neck tendons taut, for a gem like that one, the same size as that one. And finding not one, ever. Most of them, the best of them—it was easy to see from the design and the very bright colors—were just cut crystals.

I could think of nothing to say to her. I said:

"And yes, Nelly, it is something I have thought of. To surpass the objectives of a princely education, or rather, ignore them entirely. What sense in learning a foreign language if, once within that other world or universe, you'd only be fatally drawn in again by the magnet of the Book? Better to focus on it, for it's the same in all languages, impervious—as the Commentator perversely affirms, though of course without referring directly to the Book—to the fire of translations. Constructed on the solid foundation of a universal language, a primordial speech. All nuances, all distinctions, all subtleties within it. A Theory of Everything, Nelly, a Book for all days. I don't wish for, could never have wished for a better education for myself . . ."

"*Solntse,*" she interrupted me. She went over to the window and set her hands on the frame like a bird alighting there to await her husband, who was not coming, scanning the horizon from there. "Wouldn't you like to go out for a stroll?"

And she turned toward me.

Her face.

Having stood back, the maker of that face, at twenty weeks' gestation, to study the precise placement of the cheekbones' brief elevation, the almond frame of the eyes. Rotated one second of arc downward at the inner corner and one second of arc upward at the outer, like wings. I was afraid to look her full in the face: the dangerous fascination voltaic arcs exerted on me when I was a child. But I couldn't help throwing a look at the white-hot point, the acetylene flare hurtling toward me, the nucleus of a star expanding outward in a sphere. And in the center of that sphere, birds and bands of angels.

Her throat.

The stones around her throat.

"A walk? With all my heart!"

8

Like a pair of assistant directors scouting along the edge of a steep cliff for the right location to film a scene of love and complicity against the wide-open sky. The way she gave me her hand without looking at me, placing or lodging her moccasins in the grass, her calves flexing at every step. Without turning toward me when we reached the top, both looking out, both of us educated in the same antique (or primary) painters, our eyes seeing, and my legs feeling from the air that blew in through the bottoms of my trousers and swept at her skirt, that we had arrived.

I'd imagined for a moment that I would still be telling her about the hatred I harbored against the Spaniard, that painter ("the greatest of the moderns"—in other words, a commentator), and that she would listen to me without saying a word, only to suddenly turn and present me with her lips, rapidly revolving, pivoting on the axis of her neck, her eyes shooting out sparks, transformed by the sun into diamonds.

But this was what she did: she lifted her arm and stretched out her hand so that a ray of light reached my eyes, sweeping the meadow to its right, directing that light with dizzying skill or invisible diligence; the blue, the gold of the tardy sun, the green of the plants, the violet of flowers that seemed to grow larger as the beam of light swept over them.

And, revealed and concealed by the turning blades of the sun, which was simplified like a sun in a poster, its rays slicing the air into circles, her lips drew near and revolved before me, appearing and disappearing behind the beams. Pale pink outside the ray of light, shiny red within it.

Because the gesture of extending her finger had warped the surrounding atmosphere and as this magnifying glass developed in the air around it, the blue stone on her finger began shining brighter and brighter. I had only to lean forward a bit more to analyze its chemical composition (carbon, rings of carbon) and to marvel for the umpteenth time, now very close, at its unusual size: the disproportion between the size of that gem, the size of her necklace's cabochons, and the cheesy little stones worn by Silvia of Sweden and Margriet of the Netherlands.

And along the edge of that airy magnifying glass entered the words of a long explanation that I read as if in a trance, without being able to take my eyes off its surface for a second, the words distending as they reached the edges, then disappearing—but I had no need to reread them because their meaning was not escaping me. This was not a passage to comment upon, delve deeply into, and explore in order to extract some hidden message. All was expressed and stated with utmost clarity, golden words against a blue background. Without my ever having been able, without my ever having imagined anything like that, not the slightest inkling in all that time.

And when the words about the amazing size of the diamonds, their unusual coloration and, consequently, the money and Asiatic luxury of the whole house stopped emerging, the magnifying glass vanished, and I lifted my eyes and gazed deep into hers for a long second, throwing her a gaze of astonishment. Still more air entering my chest when she nodded her head several times, trying not to lose my gaze in order to transmit in that gesture the weight and gravity of her message. Which had the contrary effect of pumping even more air into me and making me continue on my upward trajectory with irresistible momentum.

9

To journey back into the past, set myself down at that point on the **walls of time,** walk through the garden, introducing myself into that moment as a wiser man, someone with the experience and exact knowledge of having already lived through that day, the late afternoon light in which we came back from the walk, went into the sun porch, and I was about to exclaim: "Synthetic diamonds!" To go over to myself and put my index finger on my own mouth, introducing a partition into the flow of that day. So that my words would flow down the opposite slope, at a wider angle, in order to extract them from my life.

And yet, no. I did none of that, none of it happened: we stopped for a second in front of the pool like two blank silhouettes, her hair rippling, my linen shirt loose. There was a moment when we reached the house and she finally turned to me and broke her silence, resolving to let me into the secret, moving me or roughly ejecting me from the safe and peaceful time where I was moving (or floating) into nights criss-crossed by white gunfire beneath a red rain. With blinding clarity. Only there, her eyes told me, only beneath that rain could I kiss her, only if I came to meet her there, leaving the island of dry air within which I walked.

Stopped there, having come full circle: on one side, my scant monthly salary as a tutor, my commentaries on the Book, the arid landscape of Spain glimpsed through a door in a wall. And on the other side, Petya, without words, without any need to use all the words I'm expending on you, a golden woman beneath a red rain. And even more diamonds among the garden grass. Diamonds revolving octahedrally in the air. Which one would you have opened, which door? Even if you knew a tiger was lurking beyond the frame, waiting to pounce?

Butterfly Valley

Sherko Bekes | Translated by Choman Hardi from Kurdish (Iraqi Kurdistan)

Contemporary Kurdish poetry is more elaborate than English. The abundant use of simile, metaphor, abstract and surreal images make translation difficult at times. In a land where tragic events take place in silence and where the difference in temperature between the harsh winters and blazing summers can be as much as fifty degrees, poetry has to live up to, and reflect, these extreme conditions of life.

Sherko Bekes has been a major figure in Kurdish poetry for the past four decades. Despite his difficult imagery and language, his poetry has been extremely popular. He is very much a poet of resistance. He has politicized landscape, weather, birds, and animals. His poetic language is not straightforward. This, accompanied by various refer-ences to historical Kurdish events and personalities, makes understanding his poetry difficult for non-Kurds.

The poem that follows is a short excerpt from Sherko Bekes's book-length poem *Butterfly Valley*. The poem was written in the late 1980s, in the wake of Anfal and Hal-abja. During the Anfal campaign 3,000 Kurdish villages were destroyed, dozens of chemical attacks were launched, and an estimated number of 100,000 civilians ended up in mass graves. The attack on Halabja remains the most well-known gas attack on civilians in Kurdistan, partly because it was a town, not a village, where over 5,000 people died instantly.

In this long poem, Sherko Bekes, who lived in Sweden at the time, is stunned by the world's silence towards these atrocities and longs to go home and mourn the victims. He laments the repetitive cycles of Kurdish history, remembering and talking to other exiled Kurdish poets from the seventeenth century to date, especially Nali, Haji, and Mawlawi.

The book was published in Sweden in January 1991, around the same time as the first Gulf War. Following the popular uprisings in March of that year, Sherko Bekes was able to return to Iraqi Kurdistan a few months after his book was published. He read this long poem to a captive audience for over two hours. I first heard a tape recording of this reading in 1991, and even without seeing the book, I loved the poem and sought to memorize parts of it.

Despite all the difficulties with translating "Butterfly Valley" I have tremendously enjoyed working on this poem. Sherko Bekes has a few book-length poems, but *Butterfly Valley* remains my favorite. It evokes exile, flight, political persecution, and Kurdish history better than any other book I know. I hope that readers will learn to enjoy him as much as he deserves.

Original text: Sherko Bekes, *Derbendi pepoola*.
Stockholm: Apec Publishers, 1991.

به‌شێک له‌ ده‌ربه‌ندی په‌پووله‌

له‌ کوێوه‌ هاتووی؟ ئه‌ پرسن —
دیسانه‌ وه‌ هه‌مان پرسیار ئه‌ بێته‌ وه‌ به‌ تووترکێ و
خوێن له‌ ده‌نگم ده‌بێنێته‌ وه‌
وا بۆ جاری هه‌زاره‌ مین
ناوی گوڵه‌ که‌م ئه‌ هێنم
هه‌یانه‌ وه‌ک (با)یه‌ک رۆژێ
ئه‌مه‌ی دابێ به‌ گوێ یاندا
له‌ دوای ساتێک سه‌رێکی بۆ ئه‌ له‌ قێن
به‌ لاّم زۆریان له‌ بێده‌نگیا ئه‌ خنکێن
مت ئه‌ بن و ملیان ئه‌ بێ به‌ نیشانه‌ی سه‌ رسورماندن
منیش ئیتر له‌ حه‌ژمه‌ تا نه‌ خشه‌ یه‌ که‌ی
وه‌ک سیاسه‌ت چرچ و لۆچ و
پیس و دراو وه‌ کو ره‌ وشتی ده‌وڵه‌ تان
له‌ گیرفانم ده‌رئه‌ هێنم
په‌ نجه‌ ئه‌ خه‌ مه‌ سه‌ر خۆری له‌ ت وپه‌ تم

Butterfly Valley

Where do you come from? They ask me—
the question transfiguring into a blackberry
that prompts my voice to bleed.
For the thousandth time, I name my flower.
Some nod after a moment,
as if, once, the wind had carried this past their ears.
But most suffocate in silence,
their necks an exclamation mark.

Vexed, from my pocket I take out a map.
A map crumpled like politics—
torn and sullied like the ethics of nation states.
I place my finger on my divided sun.
From here, from Noah's ship I have come—
I was born by the snows of Mount Judi.

ئا لێره وه —

له ناو که شتیه که ی(نوح) ه وه من هاتووم و

له به فوی(جودی) دا زاوم

ئێوه خه ونی ڕه نگاو ڕه نگی —

نێو داستان و ئه فسانه ی کۆنه ئه یبینن

هیواتان تراویلکه یه

منیش باوکم نیشتیمانی له ناو چاویا هه ڵگرتبوو

ئه و، دارخورمای به نده رێکی

چاو خه واڵووی باکووری ئه فریقا بوو

رۆژێ گه رداوی ئۆقیانووس رایفڕاند و

له (ئۆسلۆ)دا گیرسایه وه

له بارێکی وه ک ئێره دا

شه وێکی سارد وه کوو ئێستا

دایکمی ناسی

من ناوم مارگریتایه

باوکم تا مرد

خه ونی وه کوو خه ونه کانی تۆی ئه بینیی

ئه مه قسه ی کیژۆڵه یه کی دووره گی مه غریبیی بوو

شه وێکی سارد له بارێکی سه رگه رم بووی

ناو(ئۆسلۆ)دا وای پێ وتم .

مێرگێ کوڕو کچی شه نگ بوون

Yours are bright daydreams—
daydreams from old myths and legends.
Your aspirations, a mirage.
My father also carried his homeland in his eyes,
he was a date tree on a coast,
a sleepy coast in North Africa.
Then the mutinous ocean overcame him:
he ended up in Oslo.
One cold night, in a bar like this one
he met my mother.
My name is Margarita.
Till he died, my father
had dreams like you.

These were the words of a half-Moroccan girl.
She told me this on a cold night,
in a packed bar in Oslo. They were a grove of
cheerful girls and boys; they swayed
to the rabbiting of music and lyrics.

به ده م که رویشکی

گۆرانی و مۆسیقاوه

ئه شنانه وه

منیش هه ر خۆم و شیعریکی شه رمنۆکه م

خۆم و باڵنده ی ورینه م

خۆم و دووکه ڵی جگه ره م

له سووچیکا یه ک یه کترمان ئه خوارده وه

کچی دووره گ مارگریتا تازه بووه

به مانگی ناو به فری نه رویچ

تازه بووه به هه ناسه ی هه ڵماویی ئه م شه قامانه

به حه رفیکی ئه م زمانه و

به په ری مۆسیقای ئه م (بارِ)انه

مه غریب، نیشتیمانی باوکی

لای ئه و ته نها سیّ تارمابیین

سیّ تارمابیین و هیچی تر

بیابانیّ، دارخورمایه ک وحشترئ.

I was sitting with a shy poem—
the bird of my hallucinations and myself,
the smoke of my cigarette and myself:
they devoured each other in a corner.

The mixed-race girl, Margarita, has become
the moon over the snow of Norway.
She has become the steamy breath of these streets,
a letter in this language,

the wings of music in these bars.
Morocco, her father's country
is only three images in her mind,
three phantoms and nothing else:

a desert, a date-tree and a camel.

Poems by Andrej Glusgold

Translated by Donna Stonecipher from German (Germany)

Andrej Glusgold (born 1968) moved to Germany when he was twelve years old from the former Soviet Union. The German poet Ursula Krechel remarked to me that Glusgold's coming late to German allows him to use the language with a sense of liberty not always available to native speakers. Andrej is also a photographer, and his poems and photographs share an affinity for darkly surreal images that are stark and clean (as well as an affinity for taxidermied animals). Despite this emphasis on the visual, Andrej has told me that what is most important to him is how a poem sounds. Andrej has published one book of poems in German, *Ein Mann unter Einfluss*; he lives in the Prenzlauer Berg neighborhood of Berlin with his family.

The only particular difficulty in these translations was a common one for translators, and that is the English-language title of "I love Berlin." For various reasons both historical and economic, the relationship of English to German is that of a colonizing language that the colonized can't appropriate fast enough; there is a voraciousness for English on the part of German that complicates the simple terms of colonizer/colonized. Young Germans in particular prefer English expressions because they inject a New World buoyancy to the burdens of German. Glusgold's use of the English title links Berlin to New York and the ubiquitous T-shirt logo, but it also remarks upon the hypocrisy of that quintessentially American marketing move by filling the poem with dark and unlovely images of the city. As such, the use of English is deeply ambiguous.

The first problem is, of course, technical—how to indicate typographically that Glusgold has used English here? This is one of those translation problems that is bigger than any individual translator, and the quotation marks are the most workable solution, as far as I can tell, that anyone has come up with. But the rest, including the particularities of the German relationship to English, and a Russian-German's relationship to English? Perhaps once it has been indicated to the English-speaking reader that Glusgold has chosen to use English here, he or she can imagine the rest. But in some sense it is an encoded message for a German audience, which only an introduction like this can gesture at decoding.

Original text: Andrej Glusgold, *Ein Mann unter Einfluss*. Hannover: Revonnah Verlag, 2004.

I love Berlin

Ich liebe Berlin nach zu wenig Schlaf.
Die Freude in den Wintergesichtern
überträgt sich wie Herpes.

Ich sehe meine Hände und werfe
sie den Hunden zum Fraß,
auf daß sie die Gehsteige düngen
zu blühenden Paradiesen mit Kolibris und Affen,
die sich von Baum zu Baum schwingen
und Bananen durch offene Fenster reichen.
                    Da—
ihr sollt auch nicht leben wie die Kakerlaken.

Ich liebe Berlin im U-Bahngedränge.
Jemand ist von den Klippen gefallen,
aber nur so im Spaß.

"I love Berlin"

I love Berlin after too little sleep.
The joy in the wintry faces
spreads like herpes.

I see my hands and I throw
them to the dogs to chow down on,
so that they fertilize the sidewalks
into blooming paradises with hummingbirds and apes
that swing from tree to tree
offering bananas through open windows.
                    Here—
you shouldn't have to live like a cockroach, either.

I love Berlin in the throngs of the U-Bahn.
Someone falls off a cliff,
but just for fun.

Elementarteilchen

Das geniale Kind schnallt sich die Geige auf den
    Rücken und radelt los.
Im Zoofachgeschäft hüpfen vereinzelt Kaninchen.
Auf der Wiese ein verlorener Joint.
Jugendliche hängen in den Büschen herum und
    kichern.

Stellungswechsel der Fliegen über dem Teich.
Leere Nester wie Ausguckkörbe auf Dreimastern.
Morsche Omas hüsteln und grüßen.
In den Bäuchen der Schwangeren das Spannen und
    Knacken.

Elementary Particles

The child genius straps his violin to his back and cycles
    off.
In the zoo shop, lonely rabbits hop about.
In the meadow, a lost joint.
Teenagers hang out in the bushes and giggle.

The flies change position over the pond.
Empty nests like lookouts on three-masters.
Rotten grandmas cough quietly and greet each other.
In the bellies of pregnant women, tightening and
    cracking.

Rain at the Construction Site

Ersi Sotiropoulos | Translated by Karen Emmerich from Greek (Greece)

Ersi Sotiropoulos, born in Patra in 1953, is one of the best known and most highly regarded writers in Greece today. She is also one of its most controversial: her *Zigzag through the Bitter-Orange Trees*, which in 2000 became the first novel ever to win both the Greek National Literature Prize and the prestigious Book Critics' Prize, was recently withdrawn from school libraries following an obscenity trial. (The court's actions were widely protested in Greek literary and intellectual circles, and the ruling has since been overturned.)

But Sotiropoulos by no means courts controversy; her primary focus is on the workings of language itself. Fluent in French, Italian, and English, Sotiropoulos reads widely in all three languages, and her work can readily be situated in a broader context of international fiction and poetry. While her stories are often rooted in the lived reality of her native country, she has little interest in those stereotypically "Greek" elements that provide the kind of local color American readers often expect in translated literature.

Sotiropoulos began her career as a poet, and has never abandoned her early focus on the word as the primary unit of composition. Now at work on a new novel, she is trying, she says, to strip her prose down until nothing but the absolutely essential remains. That spareness and precision present perhaps the greatest challenge to the translator of Sotiropoulos's work. Since each word carries such a particular weight, "one wrong move," as the central character of this story observes, "and [it's] over."

Indeed, as I translated "Rain at the Construction Site"—in which the simplicity of the language is matched by a simplicity of action—I found myself drawn into the same kind of obsessive rewriting that defines Sotiropoulos's method. And Sotiropoulos has been as attentive to my word choices as she is to her own. In a recent e-mail, she explained that since she has "worked and reworked each line as if it were a poem," she's intent on making sure the translation gives "the proper tone, the proper rhythm." Her observations and suggestions have been of great help in my translation of this and other stories. "Rain at the Construction Site" will appear in a volume of stories— *Landscape With Dog and Other Stories*, to be published in fall 2009 by Clockroot Books—that Sotiropoulos and I have selected from her two most recent collections.

Ersi Sotiropoulos, "Vrohi sto ergotaksio"
from *Ahtida sto skotadi*. Athens: Kedros, 2005.

Βροχή στο εργοτάξιο

Στις δύο το μεσημέρι που οι εργάτες έπιαναν πάλι δουλειά, ο Λουκάς έκανε διάλειμμα. Έπαιρνε μια μπίρα κι έβγαινε στο σκαλάκι μπροστά στην πόρτα της καντίνας κι άναβε τσιγάρο. Από το σημείο που στεκόταν μπορούσε να δει την καμπύλη του δρόμου με το στιλπνό οδόστρωμα που αγκάλιαζε απαλά τους πρόποδες του βουνού και χανόταν στο στόμιο της σήραγγας. Δεν είχε πάει ποτέ ως εκεί αλλά ήξερε ότι μετά τη στροφή ο δρόμος κοβόταν απότομα και κρεμόταν σαν ακρωτηριασμένο μπράτσο πάνω από το χείμαρρο. Λίγες εκατοντάδες μέτρα πιο κάτω περνούσε ο παλιός επαρχιακός δρόμος με τις λακκούβες και το σπασμένο προστατευτικό κιγκλίδωμα. Τα καμιόνια ήταν αναγκασμένα να τον διατρέχουν πολλές φορές την ημέρα μεταφέροντας υλικά στο εργοτάξιο.

Τους τελευταίους μήνες ο Λουκάς παρακολουθούσε την πρόοδο του έργου από κοντά. Το είχε πάρει προσωπικά το ζήτημα. Κατά τη γνώμη του η κατασκευή του δρόμου προχωρούσε, όχι όμως αρκετά γρήγορα, όχι με το ρυθμό που εκείνος επιθυμούσε. «Κι εσένα τι σε νοιάζει;» νευρίαζαν μαζί του οι εργάτες. Αργά ή γρήγορα το έργο θα τελείωνε, αυτή ήταν η φιλοσοφία τους. «Μήπως βιάζεσαι να μείνεις χωρίς δουλειά;» τον πείραζε ο εργοδότης.

Ήταν μια ζεστή ανοιξιάτικη μέρα και ξαφνικά ο καιρός άλλαξε κι άρχισε να βρέχει. Ο Λουκάς μπήκε γρήγορα μέσα κι ασφάλισε τα παράθυρα και την πόρτα για να μην πλημμυρίσει η καντίνα. Μέσα σε λίγα λεπτά η βροχή είχε δυναμώσει και μαστίγωνε τις λαμαρίνες. Οι μεντεσέδες έτριξαν και το λυόμενο τραντάχτηκε από τη βάση του σαν να σειόταν το έδαφος. Ύστερα η μπόρα κόπασε. Ο Λουκάς περίμενε όρθιος μπροστά στα ανοιχτά τάπερ με το βούτυρο και τα τυριά. . . .

Rain at the Construction Site

At two in the afternoon when the men went back to work Loukas always took a break. He would grab a beer, go out onto the step in front of the canteen door and light a cigarette. From where he stood he could see the curve in the road where the freshly laid pavement twined gently around the foothills of the mountain and disappeared into the mouth of the tunnel. He had never made it that far, but he knew that just past the curve the road stopped abruptly, dangling like a severed arm above the swollen river. A few hundred yards further down was the old road, with its potholes and sagging guardrails. The trucks had to drive over it several times a day, bringing materials to the site.

Loukas had been following the progress of the work closely these past few months. He had begun to take it personally. In his opinion the construction of the road wasn't moving fast enough, not at the pace he would have liked. "What do you care?" the workmen would bark at him, annoyed. Sooner or later the road would get built, that was their philosophy. "Are you really in such a rush to be out of work?" the foreman would joke.

It had been a warm spring day, but suddenly the weather changed and it started to rain. Loukas went inside and quickly shut the windows and the door so the canteen wouldn't flood. Within a few minutes the rain had grown stronger and was lashing the corrugated metal. The hinges creaked and the prefab shook on its base as if the earth were quaking. Then the rain let up. Loukas waited, standing in front of the open tubs of butter and cheese. He tightened the valve under the sink and hesitated, listening to the water's mournful gurgling.

In his youth, he had known better times. He had

worked for years as a waiter on the ferry line from Patras to Ancona, and had made a good living. He had gotten married and they'd had a beautiful little girl with velvety eyes and skin like sugar. One summer the captain let him take his wife and daughter on a free trip. Something had happened on that trip that he still couldn't make sense of. His wife and little girl disembarked to go shopping in Ancona and never came back. Three months later he got a letter postmarked La Spezia, asking for a divorce. That was ten years ago and he hadn't seen either of them since.

There was still an hour and a half before the shift would be over and Loukas was wondering if it was worth it to wait. The flashes of lightning on the horizon had grown more frequent and a screen of mist now hid the construction site, the machinery, even the crane. The curve of road at the base of the mountain was completely invisible. Then the rain stopped as suddenly as it had begun. Everything around him was mud. He gathered his things and locked the canteen. He put the key in his pocket and started walking gingerly, careful about where he put each foot.

❊

A few weeks earlier his daughter had called. She was sixteen years old and in high school. He was dying to know how she had gotten his number and whether she had called entirely of her own accord, but he didn't ask. He learned that his wife had remarried, a man named Claudio who had a butcher shop, and that they all lived together in La Spezia. He didn't dare ask if Claudio had been the one to take them from Ancona. The lines of communication were still fragile; he didn't want to put pressure on the situation. One wrong move and it would be over. But if he was careful, he might convince his daughter to see him; he could go to Italy, or she could come to visit him that summer. Since then they had talked twice more.

"I'll tell you a story," he'd said during their last conversation. "When you were little, you were always getting the hiccups. Your mother and I were very young and didn't know anything about babies, so it worried us. We would pick you up and walk with you through the house until the hiccups stopped. Once your mother started crying because she was scared you might stop breathing and I took you down to the harbor. I showed you the seagulls, the boats, and explained all about them . . ."

"Then what happened?" his daughter broke in impatiently.

"The hiccups stopped."

"That's the story?"

"Yes," Loukas replied, with the vague impression that his daughter had been expecting to hear something different.

A Ford Fiesta was stopped at the edge of the old road with its hood open. A woman in a red coat and black high heels was bent over, examining the engine.

"I was trying to exit onto the Egnatia highway, but something happened to the car," she said when she saw him approaching.

"The Egnatia isn't ready yet."

The woman eyed him suspiciously. She looked about thirty-five, perhaps a bit older. Her hair had been done at a salon but it had gotten wet and little tufts were curling up on her forehead.

"That part of the road isn't done," Loukas explained.

"I thought. . . ." the woman began. "I'm in a real hurry," she added with a sideways glance.

Loukas leaned over to look. He didn't know much about engines, and his first impression was of a gaping abdomen with the guts all mixed up; the battery seemed to be in the wrong place and he noticed a little spiral-shaped wire sticking out.

"Is there a flashlight?" he asked.

The woman shook her head.

The end of the wire was glowing and Loukas fumbled around blindly trying to figure out where the other end led. The wire came loose without his even pulling it and lay there in his hand like a tiny snake.

"It doesn't matter," the woman said, though from the expression on her face it was clear she was on the verge of collapse. "I'm in a real hurry," she muttered again.

Fat raindrops started to fall, and again lightning tore through the sky on the far side of the mountain.

"What if we were to smoke a cigarette?" the woman suggested.

Loukas wasn't sure if she wanted his company or was just feeling hopeless. They got into the car and pulled the doors shut.

"I have an appointment and I'm very late," she said. She bit the filter of her cigarette and sighed.

Loukas took his cell phone from his pocket.

"The problem is, I can't call," the woman said. Then she was silent, watching the rain falling against the windshield.

He hadn't managed to find out much about his daughter's life in Italy. Mostly she asked the questions and Loukas answered. Sometimes her questions were so specific that he suspected they had come from her mother. His daughter wanted to hear details about his life and work, how he spent his days, and most of all who he saw.

"Yesterday a Chinese guy came by."

"You're kidding."

"No, it's true."

"Did he get a sandwich?"

"Of course."

"And to drink?"

"A coke and a bottle of water. But I lost lots of customers because of him," Loukas said, and explained that as soon as the Chinese guy showed up, all the workmen disappeared because they were afraid of some kind of pneumonia that had broken out in Asia just then. The Chinese guy didn't pay them any attention and ate a double egg and sausage sandwich. He spoke broken Greek and said he was a reflexologist from Bangkok.

"Bangkok is in Thailand."

"Then he was Thai," Loukas said and laughed nervously.

"Then what happened?"

Loukas had exhausted that episode. "A nun came once," he said, hoping to continue the conversation.

"I don't believe you."

"Yes, she was a young nun who had studied literature."

"And what was she doing in the middle of the road?"

"I don't know," Loukas said. The nun had parked her car, an old station wagon, in precisely the spot where he was now sitting with the woman, and had walked over to the canteen, her habit blowing in the wind. She was very young and cheerful but he had been in a bad mood that day and didn't feel like talking.

"Well, bye," he heard his daughter saying.

"Wait a second," Loukas said, and immediately regretted it when he heard the pleading tone in his voice.

"I have to hang up," the girl said.

That had been ten days ago, and she hadn't called again since.

The woman took off her red coat and folded it carefully over her knees. Then she moved it to the back seat. "Now what do we do?" she asked.

"We could call a tow truck," Loukas suggested.

"It's too late," the woman said, drumming her fingers on the steering wheel, "there's no point."

"I could go over to the site and see if anyone there knows about engines."

"Are you deaf?" the woman snapped. "There's no point, no one will be waiting for me now." Her eyes had welled with tears. She turned toward him. "I'm sorry," she said. With her right hand she squeezed his arm. "I'm sorry," she said again.

There were lots of things he didn't tell his daughter, things he would never tell her. Like the fact that the Chinese guy, or Thai guy, had turned out to be a con man and drug dealer: they had arrested him two days later and found two bags of pure heroin in the thin mattress he supposedly used for his reflexology. Or that the nun had been very pretty but also lame, with one leg shorter than the other and twisted like a rabbit's, and the workmen had made dirty comments about her behind her back.

Outside, the rain was coming down as hard as ever. Perhaps he should go. There was no reason for him to be sitting in a strange woman's car if he couldn't help her.

The woman opened her purse, pulled out a flask and drank from it. "Whiskey," she said, offering it to him.

"Thanks," Loukas said and took a long swig.

"Maybe it's better this way," the woman said, shaking her head.

"Are you married?" she asked after a while.

"I was."

"I still am," she said and shook the flask to see if there was any whiskey left. "And it looks like it's going to stay that way!" she added caustically.

Loukas didn't reply. He took the flask from her and drank, staring straight ahead. The windows had fogged up from their breath, or maybe his vision was blurry from the alcohol. He gave the flask back to the woman and wiped the windshield with the back of his hand. The woman pressed a button and the wipers started moving. The construction site and the crane appeared, topped by a halo of mist. The road slipped and disappeared into the mouth of the tunnel and the image looked to him like a postcard of a landscape blanketed in snow.

He'd always had a weak character, that was why his wife left him. There were so many things he would never tell his daughter, things he would never dare say. He wouldn't tell her that he lived in a dump and slept on a mattress on the floor or that his landlady was an old hag. He wouldn't tell her that he was very poor, or that when the road was finished he'd have nowhere to go. Or that sometimes he drank so much that he passed out and in the morning when he woke up he couldn't remember anything. Or that he had no friends, or that the few women he'd been with since her mother left had been whores.

"When will the work be done?" the woman asked.

"They plan on three more months," Loukas said, "but it might be sooner."

"Great work," she said and laughed ironically. One of her eyes wandered to the right and as she laughed her face had a funny childish expression.

"My name is Iota," she said after a while.

"Loukas," said Loukas.

❁

"Did you know that the Egnatia is an extension of the Via Appia?" his daughter had asked.

He hadn't known. "Meaning?"

"You mean you work right next to the Egnatia and you have no idea?"

He had to admit, he had no idea.

"When the Romans started building it, they had a plan in mind. They wanted to unite Italy with Greece, the West with the East, that was the plan. We learned about it in school. But of course there was always the sea in between . . ."

There's always the sea in between, Loukas repeated in his head. For an instant his daughter's words assumed astronomical dimensions and made him feel a kind of vertigo, an emptiness in his stomach.

"Hold me," the woman said, and Loukas obeyed. With his free hand he felt in his pocket for the key to the canteen. If the woman decided to stay with him, they could sleep there, cramped as it was. In the room he rented the landlady didn't permit guests.

Nothing happened, but the woman started to cry with little dull sobs. Her shoulders shook and she hunched up like a puppy as he held her. She was warm and unbelievably soft in his arms and her hair smelled of iodine or sulphur, something pungent and sharp.

"I'm sorry," the woman whispered, starting to pull away. "It's nothing, it just comes over me every once in a while."

"It's okay," Loukas said. "Cry if it does you good."

He held her tighter and felt calm.

He didn't want to have any expectations, any plans for the future. He didn't want to hope for something that wouldn't happen. The road would move forward on its own behind the mountain without his seeing it, and one day the severed arm would emerge from the tunnel, whole.

Poems by Anna Szabó and Krisztina Tóth

Translated by George Szirtes from Hungarian (Hungary)

Anna T. Szabó and Krisztina Tóth are both of the generation that came into adulthood around the landmark year of 1989. Szabó, the younger of the two, was born in Transylvania, and moved to Hungary from Romania, along with the rest of her family, at the age of fifteen in 1987. Conditions in Romania were dreadful, particularly for the Hungarian ethnic minority. Nicolae Ceausescu, who had been running the country since 1967, had turned it from a potentially wealthy state into a desperately poor one, where one in fifteen people was reputedly part of the fearsome *Securitate*, or security police. It was particularly hard for Hungarians because Transylvania had been under Hungarian jurisdiction for centuries, but suddenly Hungarian-language universities as well as Hungarian culture and rural communities constituted a threat. That threat lies under the surfaces of Szabó's poems—and runs fiercely, too, through the novels of her husband, and fellow ex-Transylvanian, György Dragomán.

Szabó attended school in the provinces and moved to Budapest to study Hungarian and English, obtaining a doctorate in English Renaissance and Baroque Literature. She also translates into Hungarian, and has worked on Joyce, Plath, Yeats, and Updike. Her own five volumes of poetry have brought her every major Hungarian literary prize. Her poems make little, if any, direct reference to Transylvania; rather, they are metaphysical, concerned with love, passion, and more recently, birth.

In this respect Szabó is not unlike Tóth, although Tóth, who is five years older and of a Budapest background, writes love poems with a more disillusioned bitter, haunted edge to them. Like Szabó, she was influenced by of one of the major Hungarian poets of the last thirty years, Zsuzsa Rakovszky, whose nervy urban formalism, social awareness, and colloquial voice have opened possibilities for a number of younger writers, particularly women, who, for the first time in Hungary, are among the leaders of their generation. Tóth trained originally as a sculptor, then studied history, and later worked in Paris. Like Szabó, Tóth has won every major Hungarian literary prize. Her first book appeared when she was only twenty-three, drawing immediate attention.

Szabó's poem "This Day" resembles her other work in that it is worked through sections, closely developing a theme in which intimacy and fragility maintain the chief tension. It has a firm but light hand with rhyme and meter, both of which are an essential element of the poem as meaning in that the making of a pattern is vital. She has learned something from Attila József, too, in the way she charges ordinary life with significance. The translation of the poem offered formal difficulties but little in terms of narrative or the nature of the feeling.

Tóth's poem "Dog" is altogether darker and more complex, though not unusual in terms of temper and approach. Like Szabó's poem, it takes a formal route by way of rhyme but works somewhat against pattern. There are ambiguities in the poem that are difficult for the translator. It is never absolutely certain, for example, whether the couple takes the dog home or simply remembers the dog's haunting image. The dog is also key to the sexual mood of the poem. Sex and death, and haunting and responsibility, work together to make a disquieting experience.

Original text: Anna Szabó, "A mai nap" first published in *Holmi*, issue 4, 2005. Krisztina Tóth, "Kutya," from the collection *Magas labda*. Budapest: Magvető, 2009.

A mai nap

„Ahol én fekszem, az az ágyad"

Képzeld, mi történt. Kora délelőtt,
amint utaztam új lakást keresni,
és azon tűnődtem, hogyan tovább,
míg üres szemmel bámultam a boltok
januári, kopott kirakatát,
és annyi minden eszembe jutott—

hirtelen tényleg csak a semmit láttam:
a házak közül épp kirobogott
a villamos, a hídra ráfutott,
s a megszokott szép tágasság helyett
köd várt a láthatatlan víz felett—
döbbenten álltam.

Köd mindenütt: a szorongás maga
ez a szűk, hideg, fehér éjszaka;
éreztem, hogy most ez az életem:
hogy gyorsan megy, de nem én vezetem,
hogy megtörténik, de mégsem velem,
hogy ott a látvány, s mégsem láthatom,
hogy sínen megyek, biztos járaton,
de hídon: földön, vízen, levegőben,
és felhőben is, mint a repülőben,
s a valóságnak nincs egyéb jele,
mint kezemben a korlát hidege.

Két hosszú perc, míg újra volt mit látni.
És most úgy érzem, megtörténhet bármi.

This Day

"Wherever I lie is your bed"

Imagine this. It was early afternoon
and I was on the road seeking a new apartment
wondering as I went, what next to do,
while staring vacantly at January stores
their worn-out goods, their seasonal display
and thought of many things along the way—

suddenly everything vanished:
the tram clattered between the houses, over
the bridge, and instead of the broad
vistas of river and road
dense fog hung over invisible water—
I stood astonished.

Fog everywhere: anxiety was a tight
cold sleepless night;
that's my life I thought and felt it glide
swiftly away but I wasn't part of the ride;
my life went on without me inside.
I felt it all but saw nothing anywhere
of the rails I was speeding safely on
across the bridge, on water, ground or air,
in the clouds or a plane high above land
with all assurance of reality gone
but for the cold metal barrier in my hand.

Nothing new then for two long minutes, no less.
And anything might happen now I guess.

2

Hogy folyt a könnyem! Nem tudtam, mi van,
csak feküdtem alattad boldogan.
Egy másik város, egy régi lakás.
És ezután már soha semmi más.

Elvesztettem, de megtaláltalak.
Csak azt vesztettem el, mi megmarad.
Nem az ég nyílt meg, hanem az ölem.
Jöttél az úton, indultál velem.

3

Levágott hajad sepregetem össze.
Tizenhat éve együtt. Hány helyen.
Terek, lakások. Nézegetem: őszül.
Jaj, életem.

Szemétlapátra. Hogy lehet kidobni?
Inkább szálanként összegyűjteném.
Jó, tudom: soha semmit sem dobok ki.
De hát: enyém!

Fenyőtűk közte. Nyáron napraforgó
pöndör szirmai. Hogy hull minden el.
Forog a föld is velünk, körbe-körbe.
Nem érdekel.

2

How my tears flowed! I couldn't tell why they flowed
I simply lay beneath you, bearing my load
Of happiness. Another apartment. Another town, then
Nothing after it, nothing ever again.

I lost that but found you. I lost no more
than what remains. It wasn't heaven's door
that opened but my body. So we meet.
You come and we make our way along the street.

3

I sweep up the waste cuttings of your hair.
Sixteen years together, everywhere.
Squares and apartments. I note a few grey strands.
My life lies there.

Into the pan with them. Can they be for disposal?
I'd sooner collect them all, however fine.
Yes, yes I know, I don't throw things away.
But, well, they're mine.

Some pine needles among them. In summer
light sunflower petals. How things drift and fall.
The earth continues spinning. Does it matter?
No, not at all.

4

Nem érdekel csak a nyakad, a vállad.
Ahogy megyünk egy téli hídon át,
összefogódzva. Ahogy hazavárlak.
Csak vándor hordja hátán otthonát.

Nem érdekel, hogy hol leszünk, csak együtt.
A csupasz padlón, széken, asztalon.
Én nem akarok igazán, csak egyet,
de azt nagyon.

5

Képzeld, mi történt. Érzem, hogy öregszem.
Házunk a várunk, így gondolkozom.
Pedig nem kősziklára építettünk,
hanem utazunk, egymás melegében,
a ködös hídon, egy villamoson.

És azt érzem, hogy megtörténhet bármi,
mint akkor, ott, az első éjjelen.
Pedig csak sín visz. Köd van. Ki kell várni.
Ahova te mész, oda jöjj velem.

ANNA SZABÓ

4

Who cares what happens: your neck and shoulder alone
interest me as we cross the bridge in the snow
clutching each other. I will expect you home.
Only tramps take their houses with them wherever they go.

I don't care where we are as long as we are together.
A bare floor, a few chairs and a single table.
There's only one thing I desire, no other,
but that one thing is indispensable.

5

Imagine this. I feel myself getting older.
Our home is a fortress: that's the way I am,
Though the edifice is not founded on rock.
Instead we're travelling in each other's warmth
Across the fogbound bridge with its tram.

And anything might happen now, I suppose,
the way it did that first night there, back then.
Though there are only rails and fog. Who knows.
Wherever you go now, come with me again.

Kutya

Fekete földrögnek tűnt, az olvadáskor
hegyoldalról leomlott hókupacnak.
Sötétedett, nem látszott más a tájból,
csak ónos földek, párás volt az ablak,
ahogy közeledtünk, úgy tűnt, mintha mozogna,
mintha egy kabát emelgetné a karját,
egy árnyékstoppos az útszélre dobva,
amin fényszórók tekintete hajt át.
Hol felvillant, hol eltűnt, de a sorban
odaérve mindenki kerülőt tett,
nézni kezdtem az útpadkát, hogy hol van,
és egyszer csak ott volt. Mint egy merülő test,
a mellső két láb támaszkodott a sárban,
mintha indulna, orrát a szélbe tartva,
a felső rész figyelt. De mögötte, láttam,
péppé roncsolva terült szét az alja.

Dog

It seemed no more than a clump of earth in the thaw,
a snowball that had rolled down a steep slope.
The day was darkening, nothing to see at all
just fields like tin, the windscreen part steamed up,
but as we neared it seemed vaguely to shift
like a heavy coat raising a loose sleeve,
a ditched hitchhiker's shade thumbing a lift
in the brief glare that passing headlights weave.
It was there one moment, gone the next. Each car
in the queue steered well clear of the thing
but I looked out for it on the hard verge
and suddenly there it was. It was propping
itself up on its legs, the nearside ones in sludge
as if about to run, its nose held to the air,
its upper part attent. But behind I saw
its lower half, wrecked to a pulp. And there,

A véres szőrből kiálló hátsó lába
egyenletes, kínos ütemre rángott,
ült a fél kutya, nyitva volt a szája,
és láttam a szemén, hogy mindent látott.
Kiabáltam, hogy állj meg, húzódj félre,
könyörögtem, hogy mentsd meg, üsd el,
    bármi,
vagy legyen mögöttünk már valaki végre
aki ráhajt. De hát mit kell csinálni?!
Mit kell csinálni?—emelted föl a hangod,
mit akarsz tőlem?! Mégis, mit akarsz tőlem?
Azt akartam, hogy állj meg és ne hagyd ott,
ha megtaláltad vagy vedd fel, vagy öld meg.
Egész héten ott volt a kutya köztünk.
Arra gondoltunk, jobb volna mégis otthon.
Mintha mi volnánk, akik az útra löktük,
és szavakkal kéne kerülgetni folyton.
De mégse tudtam nem akarni, hogy este
fölém hajolj: feszülő karodat néztem,
próbáltam nem gondolni a testre,
ahogy ott támaszkodik az árokszélen,

from its blood-clotted coat, stuck its back leg
that to a regular, agonising pulse kept kicking;
mouth wide open, it sat there, a half-dog
though I could tell from its eyes that it saw everything.
I cried out, Stop! draw up at the side
of the road. I begged you to save it or kill it now,
anything, let the cars behind us provide
an ending. But what can I do? What? Just how
should I end it? And so your voice grew sharp.
What do you want of me? What is it you want?
        Tell me!
I wanted you not to leave it, I wanted you to stop.
Once you found it you should look after it or kill it.
A week we tended the dog, because we thought
at least it's better off home with us giving it attention,
as if it were we ourselves who had hit it and left it out
in the road, a fact we had somehow not to mention.
But I could still not help wanting you wrapped
about me at night: I watched your muscular arm,
trying not to think of the body that lay propped
in the roadside ditch, of the leg beating like a drum

arra az ütemes mozgásra, miközben
a szemed a távolba néz és nem felel,
hogy mennyi, mennyi ádáz lemondás
van abban is, ahogy szeretkezel,
ahogy azt kérdezed, mégis mit akarsz tőlem,
miközben ütöd a kormányt és rám se nézel,
és látni a vállad mögött a szitáló esőben
ázó tájat a véres, téli éggel.

KRISZTINA TÓTH

while your eyes were focused somewhere far away
but did not answer; about the constant fury
and resignation involved in even love-making, and the way
you asked me just what it was that I wanted you to do,
striking the steering wheel over and over again,
and not once looking directly at me, while I
watched as beyond your shoulder rain beat down,
soaking fields under the bloodshot winter sky.

La Dame blanche

Christian Bobin | Translated by Alison Anderson from French (France)

Christian Bobin is a difficult author to categorize by Anglo-Saxon literary standards. He has been hugely successful in France, some of his short works selling up to 100,000 copies, and yet his books are hardly blockbusters or novels with literary heft. Rather, they are delicate, extended prose poems, ranging from reflections on life, death, art, and literature (*Une petite robe de fête, L'inespérée*) to whimsical biographies of exceptional individuals (*Louise Amour, La folle allure*). He has been writing since the mid-1980s and is an author who shuns attention or publicity, rarely giving interviews and living a reclusive life in the small town of Le Creusot in eastern France where he was born.

The excerpt that follows is, typically, neither fact nor fiction, neither prose nor poetry, but a combination of all four. Bobin is a great admirer of Emily Dickinson and this small book, *La Dame blanche*, his most recent publication, is a tribute to the "lady in white" from Amherst. It is not a biography, but rather a poetically imagined account of her life that leaves one with an impression of knowing the poet both through her poetry, as recalled by Bobin, and through his poetry, as he senses the person she is through her work and the sparse facts we have about her life.

The difficulties peculiar to translating Christian Bobin combine the usual difficulties encountered in the translation of fiction, enhanced by the importance of the poetic element in his prose. The prose is not "carried" by the story, which might allow the translator greater latitude in choice of vocabulary or the degree to which she can stray from the original; one must struggle to maintain the poetic element which has contributed both to Bobin's success and to his own peculiar position in French letters.

With the exception of *The Very Lowly: A Meditation on Francis of Assisi (Le Très-bas)* (New Seeds, 2006), very little of Bobin's prolific output has been translated into English to date. My own translation of Bobin's 1993 collection *Une petite robe de fête* is forthcoming from Autumn Hill.

To be sure, the problem with Bobin for the English-language readership is the problem facing many foreign authors who use language the way a composer uses notes: not to tell a story but to create a work of beauty that can be read over and over for its composition, the delicate craftsmanship that went into its creation. This type of literature is undervalued in Anglo-Saxon culture when it is not strictly poetry; fiction demands a story, characters, a denouement. Bobin offers a reflection on life through his short pieces, and *La Dame blanche* is no exception. We do not so much read about Emily Dickinson through his words as experience her. I hope this short excerpt will do justice both to the rest of the book, and to his prose as a whole.

Original text: Christian Bobin, *La Dame blanche*. Paris: Gallimard, 2007.

La Dame blanche

Peu avant six heures du matin, le 15 mai 1886, alors qu'éclatent au jardin les chants d'oiseaux rinçant le ciel rose et que les jasmins sanctifient l'air de leur parfum, le bruit qui depuis deux jours ruine toute pensée dans la maison Dickinson, un bruit de respiration besogneuse, entravée et vaillante—comme d'une scie sur une planche récalcitrante—ce bruit cesse : Emily vient de tourner brutalement son visage vers l'invisible soleil qui, depuis deux ans, consume son âme comme un papier d'Arménie. La mort remplit d'un coup toute la chambre.

À cette époque les familles aisées ont coutume de concurrencer l'éternel en prenant une photographie de leurs morts. Il n'y aura pas de portrait ce jour-là, juste quelques paroles soulagées des intimes et leur étonnement devant la vive blancheur du visage d'Emily, semblable à la lumière qui sort à flots d'une fleur de lys.

La poésie est la fille infirme du ciel, la silencieuse défaite du monde et de sa science. Le docteur Bigelow ne délivrait ses ordonnances qu'après avoir entrevu sa patiente allongée sur son lit, habillée de blanc. Interdit d'entrer, il établissait son diagnostic en restant sur le seuil de la chambre. Emily avait cinquante-cinq ans. Personne dans la ville d'Amherst n'a vu son visage depuis un quart de siècle.

La guerre des vivants ne s'arrête jamais : Susan, belle-sœur adorée d'Emily, vivant à cent mètres de là, n'assistera pas à l'enterrement car son mari Austin, frère d'Emily, y a invité sa maîtresse, Mabel Todd. Avant qu'arrive le couple adultère, Susan revêt Emily de son ultime armure blanche puis elle se retire. Le blanc de la robe mortuaire fraîchement repassée éclabousse la pénombre de la. . . .

The Lady in White

Shortly before six o'clock in the morning, on May 15, 1886, just as the song of birds in the garden bursts forth, rinsing the pink sky, and just as the jasmine blesses the air with its perfume, the sound stops, the sound which for two days has ruined any reflection in the Dickinson home, a sound of gasping, labored, valiant breathing, like a saw rasping over a stubborn plank. Emily has suddenly turned her face toward the invisible sun which, for two years, has been consuming her soul as if it were a frail incense paper. Death fills the entire room, all at once.

This is an era where affluent families are in the habit of competing with the Eternal by taking photographs of their dead. There would be no photographs that day, only a few relieved words from those who were close, and their surprise upon seeing how white Emily's face was, similar to the light which pours forth from a lily.

Poetry is the sickly daughter of the sky, the silent defeat of the world and its science. Dr. Bigelow did not write his prescriptions until he had seen his patient lying in her bed, dressed in white. He was not allowed to go into the room, and would make his diagnosis while standing on the threshold. Emily was fifty-five years old. No one in the town of Amherst had seen her face for a quarter of a century.

The war of the living never ceases: Susan, Emily's much-loved sister-in-law, who lives a hundred yards away, will not attend the funeral, because her husband Austin, Emily's brother, has invited his mistress, Mabel Todd. Before the adulterous couple arrives, Susan dresses Emily in her final white armor, then withdraws. The whiteness of her freshly ironed mortuary gown splatters the darkness of the green-shuttered room. For years Emily has raised a fence of white linen between herself and the world. In the library on the ground floor is Tennyson's *Saint Agnes' Eve*, with her own notations. It is the story of a nun, "in raiment white and clean," waiting for her "Sabbaths of Eternity." A timepiece deep in the sky has stopped ticking. Hiding behind death, a woman who has never harmed another waits in her robes of snow for what will happen next.

She is laid carefully in a white coffin then taken down to the hall in her father's home. The door is open onto the sun-struck garden. Dozens of butterflies lighten the suffocating blueness of the sky. Golden drones—Emily had wrenched them from their destiny of slaves by crowning them in her poems—hum a requiem for her.

Emily's sister Vinnie places two heliotropes with fragrant white flowers in the dead woman's crossed hands, "to be given to Judge Lord," whom Emily loved. On the lid of the closed coffin are several fresh violets, and ferns with their crinkled serenity. The pastor of Amherst reads a psalm, Reverend Jenkins expedites a prayer, and Colonel Higginson, the chilly discoverer of Emily's genius, recites Emily Brontë's last poem, which opens with a declaration of dauntlessness in the face of the darkness: "No coward soul is mine." As an adolescent Emily Dickinson recited this poem to her sister in the darkness of their room, before going to sleep:

"There is not room for Death
Nor atom that his might could render void
Since thou art Being and Breath
And what thou art may never be destroyed."
Nothing else will be said.

Six Irish servants, some of whom used to help Emily with her work in the rose garden—Dennis Scanlon, Orven Courtney, Pat Ward, Dennis Cashman, Dan Moynihan and the one Emily called "the gracious stable boy," Stephen Sullivan—hoist the coffin onto their gnarled shoulders, go through the rear door, whose shutters opened wide against the brick wall are like wings, and after they have made their way through the barn and its gold-striped shadows they stride into the tall grass buzzing with insects, all in accordance with Emily's instructions for the day of her burial: they must go to the cemetery through the fields, without using the street.

"When it shall come my turn, I want a buttercup." Emily's wish has been fulfilled: the field behind the house is ablaze with thousands of buttercups. The field belongs to the Dickinsons: even in death she does not leave her home, and moves without transition from the writing room to the hole dug in the earth with the Amherst gravedigger's shining shovel.

A little girl is watching as the Irish giants cross the blazing field carrying a white box on their shoulders. The little girl is six years old. She is the daughter of Mabel Todd, Emily's brother's lover. Her mother is there, in the procession. The child—her name is Millicent—watches the mourners as they walk unsteadily beneath the cynical sun, moving slowly toward the cemetery where a piece of earth has opened its gaping jaws, ready to swallow the wood of the coffin, and the flesh of the dead woman.

Little Millicent cannot stand her mother's affair. In her suffering she pictures the Dickinsons in the stormy colors of characters in a tale: walking behind the coffin are "the witch," Vinnie, with her gnarled arms "like the bundles of firewood in the logpile," and "the king," Austin, whom Millicent has often seen in her own home, frowning, seated by the fireplace with his mistress, kindling the flames with his cane, the knob of which is "a golden head."

At the age of six you have your nose glued to the window of what is real. You can see only a few details, your breath creates too much mist. Of Emily, Millicent has few images. The little girl recalls a mysterious redheaded lady in white who never left the house. From time to time a shutter would open slightly in the upstairs bedroom and the lady would lower a wicker basket on the end of a rope, and in the basket, piping hot from the oven, there would be gingerbread for a little neighbor.

The only favor the world ever showed Emily was to award her, in October, 1856, the second prize for her rye bread at the Amherst fair. The perfect word, each time it is found, illuminates your brain as if someone had pressed a switch inside your skull. Writing is its own reward.

You are fifty-five years old. You hide your face as much as you can, you would like to be seen only by God since you cannot be seen by your mother, then you die, and the first child who comes along watches, unmoved, as your coffin weaves its way across a meadow electrified with bees. There is always a stranger watching our death, and the carefree regard of our witness makes our passing a peaceful event, wearing its Sunday best, an event granted to the enigmatic procession of simple days.

Pines and ferns provide shade for the Dickinson family plot in the cemetery. Flowers are scattered over the coffin the moment it is lowered into the grave, and then everyone leaves. The heliotropes in the dead woman's hands shine in the dark.

A few hours go by, hours that are nothing. Time does not enter the home of the dead. A sun bursts noiselessly inside the coffin where suddenly it is brighter than at noon.

Fifty-three years earlier the sky above Amherst is clouding over, as at Christ's death. A storm bursts while a car-riage is passing through a pine forest. Lightning peppers the trees, the devils behind the deluge bombard the roof of the carriage, and it is forced to come to a halt. Inside is little Emily, two and a half years old: her mother, about to give birth to Vinnie, has just sent Emily to spend a month with her aunt Lavinia. The child looks out at the apocalypse and begs her aunt: "Take me home to my mother, take me home to my mother." Dying soldiers call out like this and no one answers them. Nor does anyone answer the little two-and-a-half-year-old war-rior lost on the battlefield of the world. Then suddenly, huddled in the corner on the leather seat, she becomes supernaturally quiet. "If you do not swallow your death and your fear all at once, you will never come to anything good," says Saint Teresa of Avila. That is what the aban-doned child has just done: her terror of the tons of water, her mother's irreparable silence—she has just swallowed them all at once. The devils depart to shake their fists elsewhere; the sky is shining admirably, the journey can continue.

There is a piano at Aunt Lavinia's house. The notes

which emerge are like cherry blossom petals: atoms of light cleansing the air, cleansing one's heart. Emily is allowed to run her fingers over the keyboard. From time to time she speaks about her parents and "little Austin" but shows no wish to see them. Between absence and death there is no difference. She has lost all her loved ones and wears her mourning bravely, trying not to be a burden. She is not a problem except one Sunday, they take her to worship and she talks too loudly, earning a slap. The black baptism of abandonment has made Emily as invulnerable as the dead. When you have lost everything, you can save everything. In her presence souls ignite like rosebushes: she radiates such tranquility in the evening, when it is time for bed, that her aunt likes to lie down alongside her for a few minutes—as if robbing a saint of her poor peace, touching a patch of her gown.

Aunt Lavinia, when sending news, writes that the child "runs up to me at the slightest care." Later Emily will confide with angelic brutality that she never had a mother and that she "supposes" a mother is "someone you turn to when something is tormenting you." It is the perfect definition of a mother. One never knows a thing better than when it is not there.

Edward Dickinson has a wooden head, a forward-thrusting chin, two black eyes that search and judge and convict you but which, in the end, have never looked at you. They are Old Testament eyes. The Bible is a fisherman's hut on the banks of the Eternal. There are two rooms. In the first, the father is holding a slate where he notes down all our omissions. In the second, the son is holding a sponge to wipe the slate clean. One Sunday morning, as the family is standing to attention, ready to proceed royally along the path to church, The God of the Old Testament notices that Emily is missing: not until one hour later is she found, in the cellar, reading a book whence a light clearer than that of an Easter morning arises—one of those books like *The Confessions of an Opium Eater* that Edward has bought for his daughter, warning her all the while not to read them, for fear they might trouble her. Emily's father is the type of man on whom the world rests, capable not only of providing for his family's comfort but also of governing a faraway province and of ensuring that three crosses have duly been delivered to Golgotha for Friday afternoon, as requested by the imperial administration he serves with such impeccable devotion. Treasurer of Amherst College, lawyer, senator: the medals dangling from his name jingle with every step he takes. He can imagine no salvation outside of a sleepless toil. "I expect no pleasure elsewhere than in the commitment of my soul to business. Let us prepare ourselves for a life of rational happiness": in this way he woos his wife. In his soul he is a man of law. Nothing, to his way of thinking, can ever be made clear enough. In the evening, when he opens his door to guests, he waves a lantern in front of their faces, although there is always a lamp lit in the entryway. When he converts to the new church, the minister notices this soul with its excess of polish: "You approach Christ as a man of law—you ought to go as a sinner, rather, on your knees." A Dickinson, on his knees? He prefers to plant his legs firmly on the ground and, with one hand acting as a visor, scan the skies in search of the copper

plate mounted at each corner, where the name of the Eternal has been etched along with the list of his honorary titles.

Life's footbridge creaks under young Emily's step: death, in 1852, has poached many souls around her, striking a blow to the neck then stuffing them still warm into its game bag. Some were close friends of Emily's: Abby Haskell, nineteen years of age; Jennie Grout, twenty-one; Martha Kingman, twenty-one. Emily steps quickly across the footbridge; it creaks uneasily. The following year, death will devour a regal dish: Benjamin Newton, her father's secretary. Benjamin is nine years older than Emily. He has spoken to her of the sweetness of invisible things; he lends her books and encourages her to write. She calls him "master," thus awarding him the royal ermine of a title she always confers upon men older than herself and in whose presence her sovereign soul flirts with abdication. But there are no masters before death. "I had a friend, who taught me Immortality—but venturing too near, himself—he never returned." When Benjamin collapses, the flame he had been holding and which illuminated Emily's soul rolls into the void.

That same year, thanks to her father's tenacity, Amherst was at last linked by rail to the other towns in the region: the entire village gathered at the station to celebrate the arrival of the iron horse with its nostrils of soot. The father is all-powerful, the locomotive is all-powerful, everyone is celebrating this all-powerful demonstration in order to exorcise the imminence of death. They make speeches, toss their hats into the air, shout, exult. They are drunk with progress. Emily watches her father's triumph from a distance. What became of the admirers of the locomotive, we do not know. They died even before their top hats, tossed to the sky, fell again to the dust: the hawk of the Eternal swept down upon its prey, and their naïve submission doomed them to disaster. We do know more about the contemplative woman of Amherst—we know that death would be at great pains to find her: to flee death, Emily hides behind God. Utterly in vain, of course, for God is the secret name of death. Emily knows this, but it is simply a matter of taste: either one worships the world (money, glory, noise), or one worships life (a wandering thought, the untouched wilderness of a soul, the courage of a robin). Just a matter of taste.

When Edward Dickinson has closed his accounting books, and opens the spacious register of his soul, just before he falls asleep, all he sees is a blank page: no entries, no withdrawals.

"My father sees nothing better than 'real life'—and his real life and 'my life' sometimes collide." What is "real" life? Father and daughter have two very different responses to the question. For the father, real life is horizontal: the train and telegraph are brought to Amherst, contracts are signed, men are connected to one another, and all this causes wealth to grow, to the rhythm of their exchanges. For the daughter, real life is vertical: one moves from the soul to the master of the soul—and to do that there is no need for a railroad. The only commerce is with the heavens that glow above our heads as they glow in the depths of our restraint. In such a commerce there is nothing to be earned, only a heightened sensitivity to the dried blood of Christ on the breast of a robin, as well as an understanding that grows ever finer, and therefore ever more painful, of the behavior of others.

A day comes when no one is a stranger to you anymore. That terrible day marks your entry into real life.

One day at noon, at the dinner table, Edward asks ironically, several times over, if it is "necessary" for an almost imperceptibly chipped plate to be placed before him. The third time he asks, Emily rises abruptly to her feet, takes the plate, and in the garden smashes it to pieces on a stone: may thy will be done, our father who cannot bear the sight of a single flaw in matter or in souls. Another day, outside the stable, Edward is covered in sweat, his eyes bulging, whipping one of his horses until it bleeds. He reproaches it with a "lack of humility." Emily runs over, her hair flying, and she screams at the torturer; he drops his whip and steps back, astounded. The anger of a saint is more terrible than that of the devil.

Edward has been walled up alive, like all men of Duty. Emily is aware of the dreariness of his state and, far from holding it against him, she tries to distract him: it is initially for his sake that she plays the piano and bakes the family bread, a bread so delicious that it might seem, as you break it open, that she is opening her heart. Her father praises its flavor, will eat no other and, perhaps, when chewing on a savory morsel of his daughter's bread, he has a fleeting glimpse of the child's paradise that a carefree life can bring.

The morning after her father's funeral Emily wanders like a lost child in the big cold house, crying as she enters each room: "Where is he? Emily will find him!" For two years, she dreams of him every night and writes poems so ardent that their light can be seen in the beyond—where there are no longer any roles to be played, nor positions to be held.

cold war prodigal son

Stanislaw Borokowski | Translated by Chris Michalski from German (Poland/Austria)

For an artist whose main medium of communication is the spoken word and whose performances serve, above all, to startle his audiences into a new awareness, the most surprising characteristic of Stanislaw Borokowski's poetry may be its stillness. His poems are quiet evocations of places, individuals, and events from Eastern Europe's pained recent past and the now-reunited Old World's tentative present. The main challenge for the translator of this poetry is to somehow convey the inhabited stillness of the texts as well as the unique pathos that Borokowski brings to life in them.

Born in Krakow in 1973 to an Austrian mother and a Polish father, Borokowski's identity has always spanned the poles of the two cultures and the two languages—German and Polish—in which he performs and writes. While his modest reputation rests mainly on his performances in the theater and spoken word scene in Vienna and in Poland, for more than ten years he has also cultivated a very different kind of poetry than that which he presents on stages and street corners—poems of contemplation, disaffected irony, and bittersweet remembrance. These poems, including the one published here, represent a fascinating flip side to the artist's public persona, but they are also fascinating in their own right as reflections on the Soviet past and its enduring legacy.

Common to all of Borokowski's work—and found

in "cold war prodigal son"—are the themes of exile and outsiderdom. He speaks of the disenfranchised, of homelands lost, and of human disconnectedness. Although such subjects are not new to Polish or Austrian poetry, Borokowski's background and approach set him apart from other writers of his generation, for he combines both sides of the East-West dichotomy, moving as he has for so long—as both an artist and individual—across this border, and reflecting on how this boundary has served to define lives, and how it continues to do so.

The poem presented here is from Borokowski's short volume *der halbherzige anarchist und andere texte* (the half-hearted anarchist and other poems). It's a modern reinterpretation of the Biblical parable, set during the time when the Iron Curtain still spread across Europe. In translating it I have strived to recreate the subtle emotion and sense of otherness that is characteristic of Boro-kowski's style in German. Wherever possible I have opted for straightforward, unsophisticated wording in order to bring across what I consider to be the most salient aspect of Borokowski's work—its poignant evocation of borders: the crossing back and forth across temporal and spatial boundaries, and across the line that separates the world we know from the one that lurks somewhere beyond.

Note on the translation: "Endlösung," literally "final solution," was a kind of code word used by the Nazi leadership in reference to their policy of exterminating Jews, Romani, homosexuals, the mentally ill, and other groups considered "undesirable." It is an emotionally charged word that, in the mouth of the speaker here, has an intensely personal meaning.

Original text: Stanislaw Borokowski, *der halbherzige anarchist und andere texte*. Vienna: Böcklinverlag, 2008.

verlorener sohn

wenn von einem augenblick zum anderen
der nachmittag in die dämmerung versinkt,
schleicht mein geist über den überfrorenen stausee
zum lagerhaus, wo abgelebte lkw fahrer eine
plastikflasche voll holzleim herumreichen,
schnüffelnd in das eine dann das
andere nasenloch. nur einmal brauche ich
einzuatmen und kenne den unterschied
zwischen dieser welt und der nächsten und
bin bereit für meine endlösung.

nur dass ich manchmal in meiner ekstase
glaube, ich könnte dich noch sehen, wie du
da am grenzübergang stehst, 17 jahre
alt, sprachlos und übermütig, alle abschiede
abgelehnt, voll ungeduld, dich in die eine
richtung zu drängen, um in die andere
zu gelangen.

cold war prodigal son

when almost in the blink of
an eye the afternoon dives into
the twilight my spirit slides over
the frozen reservoir to the highway
warehouse where brain-fried
truck drivers pass around
a plastic bottle of madhatters
cocktail, inhaling into one then
the other nostril. one deep breath
and i know the difference between

this world and the one below
and am ready for my *endlösung*.

it's just that sometimes in my
rapture i think i see you again waiting
at that border crossing, seventeen,
tongue-tied but fearless, goodbyes
rejected, anxious to push forward in
one direction to reach the very other.

The Words That Died in the War

Kirmen Uribe | Translated by Elizabeth Macklin from Basque (Spain)

"The Words That Died in the War" is a previously unpublished poem that Kirmen Uribe finished in April of 2007, for the PEN World Voices Festival, where he and I were presenting poems from his collection *Meanwhile Take My Hand*, published earlier in the year by Graywolf Press. In retrospect, the poem reads very much like a preliminary sketch for Uribe's autobiographical first novel, *Bilbao–New York–Bilbao*, which he was working on at the time, and which came out in Basque in November of last year. It was recently awarded Spain's Premio de la Crítica for narrative in Basque. In the novel, the grandmother of the poem—now given her name, Grandmother Anparo—remarks on the weather of the first winter of the Spanish

Civil War (mild, no snow, "as if God had wanted to soften the war, as if He'd taken pity on our fighting men"). She is startled at her own mother's desire to be buried in a castoff robe of the Virgin of Sorrows from the local parish in Ondarroa, the fishing town on the Bay of Biscay where Uribe and much of the rest of his family still live. Like the poem, the novel, too, moves through the twentieth century and into our own; and, with a character named Kirmen Uribe (b. 1970) as its narrator, it gathers other stories of the same four generations that appear in the poem, although in the novel the impact of time and history is less on words than on the people who speak them.

The insoluble difficulty of translating every single

word of this poem into English lies in its being about the words themselves. *Ardilli* is the Ondarroan pronunciation of the Spanish *ardilla* (squirrel). And, given the many years of the Franco dictatorship (1939–1975), during which Basque was banned, it makes sense that the Spanish designation would have prevailed to such an extent. (Red and yellow are the colors of the flag of Spain.) Nowadays, owing to the efforts of successive Basque regional governments, the common Basque word for squirrel,

urtxintxa, is safely in the Standard Basque lexicon, though perhaps not always in Ondarroa. Part of the pleasure of the poem itself is its rescue of the lost, local *katamixarra* (in which the *kata-* prefix does refer to cats).

The Basque *x* is a "sh" sound. The *tx* is pronounced like the "ch" in "church." The doubled *tt* affricate is far lighter than that, and, for a non-native speaker, takes some trouble with the tongue (hard against the back of your top front teeth, so a bit of breath slips past) to get it right.

Gerrarekin hildako hitzak

Hitzak ere hil ziren gerrarekin.

Hil ziren izenak.
Amonak urtxintxa esateko
zerabilen "katamixarra" hura adibidez.
"Ardilli" esango zioten umeek aurrerantzean.

Hil ziren aditzak.
Ahalerazkoak batez ere,
halakoxeak galtzen dira eta lehenik diktaduratan.

Hil ziren fonemak.
Eta errieta egiten zien amonak alabei,
aitari "atxe" deitzen ziotelako, zabar,
t bikoitza ondo ahozkatu gabe.
Ez zekitelako esaten "aitte", maitakor.

The Words That Died in the War

Words too died in the war.

Nouns died.
Katamixarra, the word our grandmother used for
urtxintxa, squirrel, for instance. The children would just say
ardilli, "squirrel," from that time on.

Verbs died.
Especially the ones in the potential mood,
that very kind gets lost first in a dictatorship.

Phonemes died.
And grandmother would scold her daughters
for calling their father *atxe*,
careless, not enunciating the double "t."
They didn't know how to say *aitte*, lovingly.

Amonaren hizkera argi dotorea,
eskuz brodatzen zituen izara zuriak bezain.
Harro eskegitzen zituen balkoian,
haizeak hegotik jotzen zuenean.
Debekatutako euskal banderaren koloreko
geranio gorri, zuri eta berdeen ondoan.

Eta errieta egiten zigun amonak bilobei,
kolore horia eta gorria bageneramatzan jantzietan.
"Franco pozik da" esanda
astintzen zituen gure haur kontzientzia txikiak.

Ezen hitzak ere hil ziren gerrarekin.
Hitzak ere bai.

Haur galtzetinak
eskegitzen ditut nik orain balkoian.
Marradunak dira, gorriak eta horiak.
Tira, badute berde pixka bat tartean.

Agurtu hala ere,
amonaren modura agurtzen naiz batzuetan;
t bikoitza ondo ahozkatu eta samur
"maitte-maitte" esanez.

Grandmother's manner of speaking was clear and bright,
elegant as the white sheets she embroidered by hand.
She hung them proudly on the balcony
when the wind blew up from the south.
Alongside geraniums the red, white and green
of the forbidden Basque flag.

And grandmother scolded us grandchildren, too
if we wore anything yellow and red.
Saying "Franco is so glad,"
she belabored our budding consciences.

For words too died in the war.
Even the words.

I hang a child's socks
on the balcony nowadays.
They're striped, yellow and red.
Or hey, they've got an intermittent stripe of green.

But to say hello and goodbye,
sometimes I do just as our grandmother did;
enunciating the double "t" to sweetly say
love you, love you, *maitte-maitte*.

The Naked Eye

Yoko Tawada | Translated by Susan Bernofsky from German (Germany/Japan)

Yoko Tawada has been a bilingual writer from the beginning of her literary career, writing both in her native Japanese and in the language of the country she's lived in for over 20 years now: Germany. Each of her books, though, has been *mono*lingual, written in either one or the other language and then, in many cases, translated into the other by a professional translator. Now she has published her first experiment in bilingual writing, the gorgeous novel *The Naked Eye*, which she wrote in both languages simultaneously. When I asked her how she wound up writing this book bilingually, she explained that she'd started it in German, but then parts of the story began to occur to her in Japanese, and so she allowed herself

to alternate between the two languages as she wrote, eventually translating in both directions until she arrived simultaneously at two finished manuscripts. The present translation is from the German. And in fact German is a thematically appropriate choice for this book, in which characters and languages are constantly being subsumed into others, with German in particular winning out over the narrator's native tongue.

The narrator of this novel, a young woman from Vietnam, travels to East Berlin a year or two before the fall of the Berlin wall in order to participate in an international Communist youth conference. There she is kidnapped by a West German student, who incorporates her into his bland life in Bochum. Her attempt to escape to Moscow—from where she assumes she'll be able to make her way home, since she speaks fluent Russian—results in her inadvertently catching a train to Paris. The Ai Van referred to in the chapter "Zig zig" is a Vietnamese woman she meets on the train.

The "you" apostrophized in this chapter and throughout the book is legendary screen actress Catherine Deneuve. The narrator quickly begins to spend all her time at the movies, developing such a fascination with Deneuve that she sees each of her movies many times even though she can't understand the French dialogue; she then relates the plots as she understands them, interspersing (and sometimes confusing) them with her own story. The result is a work of virtuoso cinematic intertextuality in which all the overlapping stories make even more poignant the narrator's feeble attempts to maintain and assert her own identity.

Perhaps the greatest challenge of translating this novel was maintaining the slight feeling of alienation in the language, which on the one hand is literary, rich and lyrical, and on the other, possessed of a slight halting quality that seems intended to remind us that the narrator is speaking a language not native to her. In another story, Tawada writes, "Often it sickened me to hear people speak their native tongues fluently. It was as if they were unable to think and feel anything but what their language so readily served up to them." Greater truth, perhaps, can be found in a language one has learned from scratch. When I was working on the translation, Tawada asked me to be careful not to make the book's language too polished in English, explaining that she considers "stumbling [. . .] one of the most important activities of a reader." Tawada's writing in German remains graceful even when it stumbles, and the smidgen of awkwardness it contains is just enough to remind us that it is language we are reading, and that communication in words is a skill that must be practiced and learned.

Original text: Yoko Tawada, *Das nackte Auge*. Tübingen: Konkursbuch Verlag, 2004.

Das nackte Auge

Zig zig

Zahllose Schornsteine ragten aus den Ziegeldächern. Einige waren kurz und dick, andere waren wie ausgemergelt. Ich nahm eine der breiten Straßen, die am Nordbahnhof begannen, und ging einfach immer geradeaus, ohne mich umzuschauen, damit ich in den Augen der Passanten zielsicher wirkte. Nur die Kreuzungen mit fünf Straßenarmen machten mich unsicher. Hier konnte ich nicht mehr sagen, was "geradeaus" genau bedeutete.

Der Vorhang wurde im Himmel langsam zugezogen, und das Wellenmuster der Pflastersteine schwärzte sich. Wer hatte sich so viel Zeit genommen, um diese Steine genau zusammenzulegen? Wie war es möglich, dass sie alle so gut zusammenpassten? An der Stelle, an der das Wellenmuster in ein Schlangenschuppenmuster überging, began es zu regnen. Ich blieb stehen, blickte zurück, die Pflastersteine waren verschwunden, und an ihrer Stelle lag eine matt asphaltierte Straße. Ich ging weiter. Die Schritte der Stöckelschuhe näherten sich von hinten und überholten mich. Ich erfuhr nichts von dem Gesicht der Frau, sondern sah nur ihren angespannten Rücken. Einige andere Menschen überholten mich ebenso: ein Mann, der den Kragen seines Sommermantels hochzog und kerzengerade ging, als würde er sonst seinen Kopf verlieren; eine ältere Dame, die mir auch einen einsamen Rücken zeigte, vielleicht hatte sie gerade ihren Pudel verloren.

Die nassdunklen Fensterrahmen erinnerten mich an die Ränder müder Augen. Ich hatte nicht den Mut, jemandem den Zettel zu zeigen und nach dem Weg zu fragen. Menschen huschten an mir vorbei, eilten zu einem mir unbekannten Ziel. . . .

The Naked Eye

Zig zig

Numberless chimneys stuck out from the tile rooftops. Some of them were short and fat, others looked emaciated. I took one of the broad streets that began at the Gare du Nord and walked straight ahead without looking around so that anyone watching me would think I knew where I was going. Only the five-armed intersections made me uncertain. Here I could no longer say what "straight ahead" meant.

The sky's curtain was slowly being closed, and the wavy pattern of the cobblestones darkened. Who had taken so much time to arrange these stones so precisely? How could they fit so neatly together? At the point where the pattern of waves gave way to a pattern of snake scales, it began to rain. I stopped in my tracks and looked back: the cobblestones had vanished, replaced by a dull asphalt street. I walked on. High-heeled footsteps approached from behind and overtook me. I saw nothing of the woman's face, only her tense back. Several others overtook me as well: a man who was pulling up the collar of his summer coat and walking bolt upright as if he might otherwise lose his head; an older woman who showed me her lonely-looking back—perhaps she'd just lost her poodle.

The dark, wet window frames made me think of rings beneath weary eyes. I didn't have the courage to show someone the slip of paper and ask directions. People flitted past, hurrying toward their unknown destinations.

A shop window filled with old miniatures depicting dogs attracted my attention. I pressed my nose up against the glass to get a better look at the miniatures and etchings. I'd never seen many of the breeds before, yet I realized for the first time in my life that I loved dogs. If I were a dog, I would immediately feel safe in any city.

The wet streets shone black as the snout of a healthy dog. Would the night eventually just swallow me up? I kept walking. The bright neon advertisements of the restaurants blurred together in the moist air. Randomly turning into an alleyway, I found a shop whose plate-glass window displayed pink, light blue, and yellow umbrellas beneath glaring lights. Behind the counter, two sales-women were arguing. One was much older than the other. Perhaps she was the other one's mother. There was a period when my older sister, too, argued with my mother on a daily basis. My mother didn't like my sister's lover. The argument reached its climax when my mother learned that my sister was pregnant. But then the argumentative phase gradually ended. When you get a high fever, your cold will soon be over—these were the words of wisdom my sister shared with me.

In another alleyway, two women stood wearing net-like stockings that reminded me of mosquito netting. One woman, whose dress was brown, had golden hair, while the other, who had chestnut brown hair, wore a golden chain. Both of them were attentively observing the passers-by on the boulevard and didn't even notice I was standing in front of them. Soon a man turned off the boulevard and approached the woman with a wobbly gait. This rather fat man, who had drawn his cap down until it all but covered his eyes, pulled some money out of his breast pocket and shook the bills before the nose of the chestnut-haired woman. To my surprise, she smiled at him, took his arm and led him into the darker part of the alley. I followed them and watched them go up the stairs of an old two-story building. Soon the light went on in one of the rooms. Apparently, the woman was renting rooms for the night. I had a few banknotes as well. Ai Van said I could easily live on this money for several days. Therefore it seemed excessive for this woman to be asking so much money for a room in this run-down building. My teacher always told us that it was a basic human right to be able to sleep beneath a roof and between four walls. Earning money by renting rooms, he said, was one of Capitalism's most grievous transgressions. If this was how people here lived though, I certainly wouldn't succeed in reeducating them overnight. It was already too late to look for the apartment of Ai Van's sister. Because of the mosquitoes I definitely didn't want to sleep outdoors. Here one could apparently get a room using sign language. I went back to the spot where the blond woman was still standing. She was so good-looking she ought to have been in the movies. Maybe she hated cameras, just like me. And who can say which is a better profession? I took out my banknotes and shook them before the nose of this woman, who was at least ten centimeters taller than me. She opened her large eyes even wider and batted her elegant, curved eyelashes. Although I hadn't done anything different than the man before me, the woman was so surprised she nearly froze. Impatiently I grabbed her by her bare upper arm, making her flinch and take a step back. I pointed in the direction of the old building where the other woman had disappeared with the man, and nodded at her, smiling. She glanced quickly at my banknotes and assumed a pensive expression. Then she searched for something between my eyes and my mouth. She appeared to find whatever it was she was looking for

as her frozen face relaxed a little. I took her by the hand and pulled her toward the entrance of the building.

A large oval mirror hung in the room. The mirror seemed to show me precisely what the woman, too, saw when she looked at me: a shy, scrawny girl. Only her eyes gleamed as if caught in a high fever, and her lips burned apple-red. Was this really me? In high school I was one of the girls who made a sturdy, mature impression. No one ever told me I was thin or looked childish. The mirror also showed the woman standing behind me. A dramatic curve descended from the back of her neck over her breasts and hips down to her thighs. A masterful brushstroke. When I turned to face her, she no longer resembled a two-dimensional work of art but rather was living matter heavy with flesh. She asked me something. I recognized the word "Papa." Perhaps she thought I was looking for somewhere to stay together with my father. I said in English, "Only for me." I always claimed not to know any English. But if I were to drum up every English word I knew, perhaps I could actually speak a little English. Was the woman afraid that without my father I wouldn't be able to pay for the room? I pressed my banknotes, which had grown somewhat moist with my sweat, into her hand. Then I had to squeeze her hand shut, because the woman was just staring at me and ignoring the money. Apparently there was something wrong with my face.

The woman sat down on the bed, and I sat down beside her. She seemed to be waiting for something. I tried to think what else one should do when renting a room. I couldn't think of anything. Perhaps she was just lonely. A bit of fuzz clung to her hair above the ear. I reached out my finger to remove it. The woman flinched as if she were afraid of me. What about my body could be so intimidating? Even if we were to quarrel and come to blows, she would be the victor. And above all: What would we quarrel about?

I remembered my great aunt who had died two years before. During the last months of her life she was afraid of things no one else could see. When I asked her what frightened her, she would say: "A soldier without legs came to see me" or "The bones buried beneath the kitchen sob at night." Once she poured cold water on herself and said her dress was on fire. She also told me that in the forest there was a charred tree stump from which headless children were born. The word "imagination" meant nothing to her, and a different word, "hallucination," was something she'd never heard. When I embraced her and stroked her cheek, her flesh would relax. She would then repeat "Thank you, thank you, thank you" and grow a little calmer.

This woman, too, young as she was, probably suffered from hallucinations like my great aunt. Out of pity I placed my arm around her neck and drew her to me. At first she tried with hesitant fingers to push my belly gently away from her. Then her fingers groped for my spine and read Braille. She asked me something I didn't understand. Maybe the meaning of the question was unimportant anyway. I couldn't comfort my great aunt with words either. Instead, one had to say yes to every question and calmly pet her. I nodded to the woman and stroked her cheek. For some reason I couldn't fathom, she pulled down the zipper of her dress, slipped out of this shell, and opened the hooks of her undergarments. Then she took my hand and pressed the tips of my fingers against her nipple, which felt like the toe of a cat. There was a tiny fissure at its center. Perhaps this fissure was where the mother's milk came out. I couldn't remember whether I too had a fissure like this. The woman seemed to have read my thoughts in my face. She unbuttoned my blouse with trembling fingers. My skin looked flat, inexpressive, shut off. Once her fingers began speaking to it, though, my skin began to open up, not just my nipples, but my whole body.

Suddenly I felt the inner wall of my stomach burning with hunger. I thought of the red of prawns shimmering through moist rice paper, or the white of steamed fish one carefully unwraps from a bamboo leaf. The woman asked me a question. As an answer, I placed my hand on my belly. The woman nodded without giving the impression she was about to get me some food. Instead, she stuck her fingers under my belly. At the same time I saw her lips in close-up, her wet teeth were gleaming between them. From her mouth drifted a smell like lemongrass, making

me dizzy. I lay down on my back, and the woman's skin blocked my vision. The white, warm skin melted on my tongue, but I didn't bite any off. I was in a round space, perhaps within a sphere. There was one fixed point on the inner wall of this sphere: the place where my temple touched hers. Both were as hard as stone, thoughtful, not melting together, waiting for something new. I was dreaming of peas. The peas were as hard as stone before they grew astonishingly soft in a pot of boiling water. I dreamt of oysters with lemon juice, eating them with a sobbing sound, my fingers taking on their fragrance.

I heard someone hurriedly unlocking the door from outside. The woman leapt up: in the doorway stood a man whose well-groomed brown hair hung down like the ears of a dachshund. The woman quickly covered us with the wool blanket while arguing hot-headedly with the man. Then she wrapped the sheet around her, got up and chased him out the door after hurling a few more explosive words in his face. From the floor I retrieved my neck pouch, which contained the money and my passport, and got dressed, while the woman, who had gotten dressed in two seconds, waited for me impatiently. Then she grabbed me by the wrist, ran out of the room and hurried down the steps. We rushed down the alley in the opposite direction to the boulevard. This was a network of dark but pleasant-smelling alleys. Eventually we arrived at the entrance to a building that looked charred. The woman didn't even have to hunt around for a light switch as her toes could clearly see the steps that led down to a basement. In the basement room the light switch was broken, but through the barred window one could see a little light reflecting off the cobblestones. Between the stacks of cardboard boxes with writing on them stood an animal with horns and a rusty bicycle. The woman sat me down on a box and pointed to the numerals eight and two on her watch. Then she left.

An old floor lamp exactly my height stood beside me. The lamp had a cable that vanished in a dark corner—a good corner for an overlooked electrical outlet, but what good was an outlet for a lamp with no bulb. A deformed leather handbag at the base of the lamp was cracked and hard. Opening its metal navel wasn't easy. I held the bag

upside-down. A crumpled, dried-up handkerchief fell out followed by lipstick, a ballpoint pen, and a flyer advertising a movie. The title of the film was *Zig zig*, and the date was already ten years in the past. This was the first time I saw your name. And this was the one film I was never able to see, even later. A long time passed before I understood that it wasn't necessarily important whether or not one has actually seen a film.

The woman was called Marie. She left the basement every evening and returned around two in the morning. When I sat alone in the basement, I felt like a hostage abducted by terrorists. The worst thing about these terrorists was that in reality they weren't making any demands and thus would never release me. Of course I wasn't locked up—I had unlimited freedom and could leave the basement if I wished.

Marie was not an abductor, she was my protector. She protected me by ignoring me. She acted as if she were unable to see me, or as if I were a wildflower that just happened to be growing in her garden. If only I'd been able to exchange just a few words with her. I couldn't understand her language, and she even seemed to be withholding it from me. When she returned from work, she would install herself in her favorite corner like a work of art for the world to see but was nonetheless unapproachable. I wouldn't have felt so useless if she had, for example, forced me to join her in her nocturnal perambulations. Or she could have threatened me with her knife and forced me to sell pears. Indeed, she possessed a double-edged knife, but she only used it to peel apples. I missed the sense of being bound to other people. Of course it wasn't right to offer up one's body—a gift from our ancestors—as goods for sale. And in any case the desire to provide a service as a way of earning money was a capitalist malaise. I remained behind in the basement, isolated and useless. If I'd had a child of my own, I'd at least have had a task. Perhaps this was the reason other people produced children. The child in my uterus had at some point vanished into thin air. Or the child existed from the very beginning merely as Jörg's phantom pregnancy.

During the day I walked around the city so as not to have to sit behind bars. The streets drove me on without a goal from one corner to the next, no armchair waited to receive my weary limbs. Be still, I said to the pavement beneath my feet, but it kept flowing on and on like a conveyor belt, and I was the automobile tire. I remembered the shoes called Ho-Chi-Minh sandals that were made from old tires. If I were to wear them here, they would be seen as a symbol not of frugality but of a ceaselessly increasing velocity.

Sometimes I saw policemen on the street. What would happen if I were to describe my situation to them and ask for help? "I let down the East Berliners who were expecting me to give a speech. I illegally crossed the border between East and West. A woman played the role of a would-be suicide to stop a train for me. From there, I traveled to Paris without a ticket. I borrowed money from a Vietnamese woman and never went to see her. I am living in a basement without paying rent. Yesterday I stole a rose from a flower vendor." If I were to tell my story freely, the policemen wouldn't help me, they'd arrest me.

Candor is incompatible with freedom. Is a person any more able to find his way home from inside a prison? What would my relatives and above all my teachers and friends have to say about this? They would no doubt start collecting money right away so that my parents could come visit me in Paris. But what a shame it would be if their first trip to Paris was to see a jailbird. Besides, they would be utterly unable to help me here. In Saigon my father knew influential politicians—connections of no use to us in Paris. When I was younger, I never needed to keep any secrets. As long as I was honest, industrious, and modest, loved my friends, teachers, and family, nothing bad could happen to me. This security was now long gone. I had become a criminal without ever having had any intention of doing wrong, and without having so much as killed a bug. Someone once told me that in Paris one could place international phone calls even from a normal telephone booth. Was there also a direct line to the realm of the dead? I would have liked to call Confucius and Ho Chi Minh and ask them what to do.

If a policeman thought me suspicious, he might stop me and ask to see my passport. I always carried my passport with me, but I had no visa for France. Fortunately my Asian features did not make me conspicuous. This city was full of Asian-looking women. Most of them were in the habit of glancing into shop windows to check the quality and prices of handbags and dresses for sale. Sometimes, to my surprise, I caught a glimpse of my own mirror image, which always horrified me. You could tell from my body language that I had no intention of buying anything in the display window. Whenever a saleswoman looked at me through the glass door, trying to figure out what brand name might be of interest to me, I would hurry away. In my eyes, these brand names were simply crooked letters, pictograms whose meaning I could not discover. Anyone could see at a glance that I had no right to be here.

To escape the agitation of the streets, I sought refuge in movie theaters. One could linger here for hours for little money. In the dark there was no danger of being observed by a policeman. My first film was Polanski's

Repulsion. On the poster for this film I discovered the name of the actress printed on the old flyer for *Zig zig*. This was why I could walk right up to the ticket window and courageously pronounce the film's title. *Repulsion* had been made twenty years before, and so my very first time seeing you was at a temporal remove.

The movie theater was even darker than the basement, though there was something reassuring about the space. On the screen strangers played out their lives for me to see. I couldn't imagine myself as a character living in Paris. For the first time, however, I could truly picture my own body in various positions. Like the first time I lay in bed in Bochum staring at the walls. I learned this from the bedroom scenes in *Repulsion*. It wasn't just me lying in bed, it was you.

Marie usually returned to the basement much later than I did. When I came back from the theater, I would rewind an invisible roll of film inside my head to watch the movie again from the beginning. My mental cinema boomed with a dull percussive sound. The characters fell silent. I saw the protagonist hurrying somewhere with long strides. Her fingers kept trying to remove something invisible from the wing of her nose. A skinned rabbit was stuffed in her handbag. Behind her armoire, a crack opened in the wall. A strange construction site in the middle of the busy street might have been a pedestrian island. An old neighbor woman wearing so many layers of clothing she appeared spherical stood at the door of the building with a hat and a dog. Three street musicians the size of children were playing accordion, clarinet, and drum. As they played, they slowly walked backward.

When I heard Marie's footsteps, all the images in my head vanished and I would greet her at the basement door. She would turn her face away from me as if in embarrassment, murmuring a few words I couldn't understand. Once I placed a delicate-scented rose I'd stolen in the city in the place where she slept. Marie ignored both me and the rose, her strong perfume stinging my nostrils like the scent of lilies in sickrooms that irritate the patients' mucous membranes and cause nightmares. A perfume war between the lily and the rose. Marie hid behind the scent of the lily. Since the night of the misunderstanding, we hadn't touched each other. I felt that Marie was trying to keep me at a distance from her profession, and had nothing else to offer me.

One day Marie came home with a book which she pressed into my hand while saying a few words in an encouraging tone of voice. The book was yellow with a large black-and-white photograph on the cover. At first I didn't recognize the woman in the picture. The word *Ecran* was printed in round letters on the cover next to two mysterious numbers: "78" and "73." Had Marie bought the book from a peddler on the street, or had a customer given it to her? I was surprised to discover a scene from *Repulsion* in the book: the main character, Carol, in the process of writing something on the surface of a mirror.

I remembered a situation I'd almost forgotten. I was standing outside, leaning against the cinema's wall as if drunk when Marie walked by and looked at me questioningly. I pointed to the poster I was leaning against. With the seriousness of a child learning to read, Marie read aloud each of the names on the poster: director, actors, actresses. When she read your name, I nodded.

At the time I didn't know that *Ecran* was a magazine and not a book. The books I'd read as a schoolgirl had been similarly bound and were as thin as this journal. *Ecran* became my first language textbook. All night long, my hot temples refused to sleep. With the help of this book, I would learn the language, then I'd study philosophy at the university, join the Party and rise among its ranks. Eventually the Party would come to power and I would become leader. I would give an apartment to every person who lived in a basement, and I too would move into such an apartment, perhaps together with Marie. We would look out our big window at a big walnut tree in which spirits liked to linger. Fresh water free of bacteria would flow out of the faucets at any time of the day. The water might smell a little like a swimming pool, but even the odor of the chlorine would seem pleasant to me as it would remind me more of my summer vacations as a child than of a hospital. In the mornings, Marie would use the subway pass distributed free of charge at the factory to ride comfortably to work, where she would don a blue uniform that she didn't have to wash herself but could simply drop off at the laundry department after work. In the evenings she would always come home on time since working overtime was illegal. Without a care in the world, she would hop in the bathtub. Of course, it would be much more fun to bathe in a large bathhouse with all our friends. But it would be fine with just the two of us as well. We would no longer eat with plastic forks and knives from plastic plates held on our laps, but instead would sit at a table and use bamboo flatware. The rats and mice that tormented us in the basement would not be found in our new apartment. They would willingly go live in the forest. Then again, I wasn't quite sure whether they did in fact come from forests or had always lived in basements. If the latter, public basements would be created for the rodents so they wouldn't have to live out in the wild.

When the sunlight shone past the window bars the next morning, I caught the glimmering light in the open book in my hands. Between pages eleven and twenty-five were sixteen photos of you: four close-ups of your face, and twelve scenes from various movies. This was the day I consciously began addressing you in the second person, although I didn't know you yet and you remained utterly unaware of my existence.

Out of your many faces I constructed a single face, and this one face differed from all the others I saw in the city. Other women's eyes could never quite capture my gaze; their noses appeared to have been artificially constructed, their mouths randomly affixed. Incidentally, I always forgot to include myself when I thought of these "other women." My person vanished in the darkness of the movie theater, and all that remained was my burning retinas reflecting the screen. There was no longer any woman whose name was "I." As far as I was concerned, the only woman in the world was you, and so I did not exist.

In the Hot Wind

Celia Dropkin | Translated by Yerra Sugarman from Yiddish (White Russia/U.S.)

Celia Dropkin, innovator of the erotic modernist love poem in Yiddish, began writing poetry in her mother tongue for the first time approximately five years after immigrating to the U.S. in 1912. She was born in 1888, in Bobruisk, White Russia, what is today Belarus. Dropkin wrote in Russian until 1917. Her earliest Yiddish poems were her translations of work she had originally written in the language of her birthplace, her other mother tongue.

Masterful in its invigoration of meter and rhyme and in its exploration of free verse, the personal lyric that establishes Dropkin's stature in Yiddish literature is groundbreaking in its candor about sex, love, death, and relationships between men and women. It addresses other subjects with immediacy: nature (often eroticized), motherhood, and childhood. By exposing desire buried in a woman's body, Dropkin takes a place in twentieth-century literature. Exploring her conflicts, Dropkin challenged preconceptions of women's poetry in Yiddish as a form of popular, non-canonical prayer. Her work, compared to Plath's, exceeds conventions even now.

Although Dropkin's poetry was acclaimed for its originality, it was disparaged by some Yiddish male critics and by her contemporaries, who found it lacking in Jewish content, as well as too erotic, personal, emotional, and insufficiently political for the leftist literary circles of the time. Nevertheless, she was a significant immigrant poet recreating Yiddish into a modern poetic language, contributing to the burgeoning of Yiddish poetry in New York from the late nineteenth-century until the beginning of World War II. The group with which Dropkin is sometimes associated, "The Introspectivists," embraced modernism, and along with three other major Yiddish groups, formed a genuinely American literary establishment, second only to their English counterpart. Dropkin self-published one poetry collection, *In the Hot Wind*, in 1935. After her death in 1956, her children oversaw the publication of a comprehensive volume that finally appeared in 1959.

Dropkin's lullaby "In the Hot Wind" reveals her obsession with transgression and also innocence as a reprieve from unmanageable passions; the speaker in such work suffers guilt because she cannot conform to the conventional life of a wife and a mother. The poem negotiates borders between illicit love, danger, and the solace derived from children. Writing as a mother contributed to Dropkin's creative energy, motivating her to recall Yiddish lullabies and the innocence to which she related. She used Yiddish children's rhymes to set a folk decency beside her concerns with the experiences of a woman's body, seen in her poem as the speaker struggles to reconcile sexual and emotional conflicts with the demands of motherhood. Dropkin juxtaposes purity and violence, recalling the paradox of "Rock-a-bye-Baby," with which her poem shares many elements: blowing wind, trees, branches, solace, guilelessness, and danger.

To blend that innocence with transgression was a difficulty posed in translating the lullaby. Balancing its lightness and darkness was attempted by sustaining the rhythms—in part two, a necessarily tumbling one, suggesting a fall, the "sin"—and her simple diction, as well as some of her rhyme, even through slant-rhyme. The unexpected and ambiguous ending posed another challenge.

Celia Dropkin's poems are a testament to Jewish women's transformation of their homely folk tongue into a lyrical language.

Original text: Celia Dropkin, *In heysen vint*. New York: Shulsinger Bros., 1959.

אין הייסן ווינט

1

אימער פֿרי

עס ווויגט דער הייסער ווינט
די פֿרישע, פֿרישע בלעטער,
ווי עס ווויגט אַ יונגע מוטער
איר ערשט קינד.

עס רוישט דער הייסער ווינט
אין די פֿרישע, פֿרישע בלעטער,
ווי עס זינגט אַ יונגע מוטער:
ליו-לינקע, מײַן קינד.

In the Hot Wind

In the Morning

The hot wind rocks
The fresh, fresh leaves,
Like a young mother rocking
Her firstborn.

The hot wind whooshes
In the fresh, fresh leaves,
Like a young mother singing:
Hush, little baby, hush.

2

בײַ טאָג

עס ווײגן זיך אין הייסן טאָנץ,

אין אָרעמס פֿון דעם הייסן ווינט,

אין זונענגלאַנץ,

מיט גרינע פֿעכערס צווײַגן,

זיי דרייען זיך אין קאַראַהאָד פֿון זינד,

צעפֿלאָכטן מיטן הייסן ווינט,

אין זונענשײַן געקליידט,

אָט ווערן זיי צעשיידט,

אָט זײַנען זיי צוריק צעפֿלאָכטן מיטן ווינט,

ווי הייס בלוט אין די אָדערן פֿון צווײַגן,

טאַנצט יעדעס בלאָט אין קאַראַהאָד פֿון זינד

עס וויל ניט איינער רוען, שווײַגן,

און טאַנצט און זינגט אַ ליד פֿון זינד.

3

פֿאַרנאַכט

געענדיקט איז דער טאַנץ פֿון זינד,

אַנטשלאָפֿן איז דער הייסער ווינט,

די ביימער זײַנען מיר פֿאַרשמאַכט,

זיי ציען, ציען זיך פֿאַרטראַכט,

צום ריינעם הימל אין דער הויך

ווי דינער, גרינער רויך.

2

In the Daytime

Rocking in a hot dance,
In the arms of that hot wind,
In the sun's radiance,
With green fans, the branches
Reel in a round of sin,
Entwined with the hot wind,
Adorned in sunlight.
One minute they're apart,
The next they're entwined again with the wind.
Like hot blood in the veins of the branches,
Each leaf dances in the round of sin.
Not one wants to rest, or be silent
And dances and sings a song of sin.

3

At Dusk

Ended is the dance of sin,
Asleep now is the hot wind,
The trees weary, languishing,
Stretch and stretch pondering
Purest heaven up above
Like thin, green smoke.

Even Summer Has Passed

Arseny Tarkovsky | Translated by Jon Jensen from Russian (Russia)

Arseny Tarkovsky (1907–1989) was the father of the legendary Soviet film director, Andrei Tarkovsky. The two represent a rare historical instance of a child gaining recognition at the same time as his or her parent. Andrei's first feature, *Ivan's Childhood,* was released in 1966, the same year as his father's first published book *Before the Snow.* Arseny was fifty-five; his son was thirty-four.

The poet's earlier book, *The Star Guests,* had been repressed by the Soviet authorities in 1946. This event was devastating to Tarkovsky, who had lost a leg serving in the Red Army during World War II. The persecution of the poet was much more cloaked than that of his contemporaries, Akhmatova, Tsvetaeva, and Pasternak, but damaging nonetheless: for many years he swore that he would never attempt to publish his work again.

Arseny eked out an existence for himself and his family publishing translations from a wide variety of Near Eastern languages: Armenian, Azeri, Georgian, Turkmen, and Arabic. Although his work gained him a degree of recognition, few but his closest friends were aware that Tarkovsky wrote at all. This further marked his sense of creative and spiritual isolation apparent in much of his work.

The influence of the elder Tarkovsky's writing on his son's filmmaking was openly acknowledged with the release of *The Mirror.* The film featured Arseny reading several of his poems, including "Even summer has passed . . ."

The father suffered greatly, however, because of his son whose enigmatic, poetic movies began to anger the Soviets at the same time they gained greater and greater acclaim in the West. In 1983, Andrei defected. Soon after, his father's work was bitterly criticized by the Russian press.

The two never saw each other again. Andrei died of cancer in 1986. The poet, Arseny, whose fame began simultaneously with his son's, outlived him by two and a half years.

The rare translations of Tarkovsky that have appeared in English often overlook the traditionality of his form, and more importantly the jarring, often surreal, shifts in content and register that often occur within his poems.

Original text: Arseny Tarkovsky, *Sobranie cochineniy v triokh tomakh*. Moscow: Khodozhestvennaya literatura, 1991.

"Вот и лето прошло…"

Вот и лето прошло,
словно и не бывало.
На пригреве тепло.
Только этого мало.

Все, что сбыться могло,
Мне, как лист пятипалый,
Прямо в руки легло.
Только этого мало.

По напрасну ни зло,
ни добро не пропало,
Все горело светло.
Только этого мало.

Жизнь брала под крыло,
Берегла и спасала.
Мне и вправды везло.
Только этого мало.

Листьев не обожгло,
Веток не обломало…
День промыт, как стекло.
Только этого мало.

"Even summer has passed…"

Even summer has passed,
Like there'd never been one.
It was warm on the porch.
But it wasn't enough.

All that might have been was,
Like a five-petalled leaf,
Placed right here in my hands,
But it wasn't enough.

The good wasn't in vain,
What went wrong wasn't wasted,
It all burned with clear light,
But it wasn't enough.

Life caught me under its wing,
It preserved and it saved me,
And in fact I lucked out.
But it wasn't enough.

Not a leaf was burnt up,
Not a twig snapped in half . . .
The day was washed like a glass,
But it wasn't enough.

Azorno

Inger Christensen | Translated by Denise Newman from Danish (Denmark)

Inger Christensen's highly original works as a poet, novel-ist, playwright, and essayist, distinguish her as one of the most important experimental writers of our time. Born in Vejle, Denmark in 1935, she lived in Copenhagen from the early '60s when she made her literary debut with Light (*Lys*, 1962). After that she published three novels, two essay collections, six books of poetry, including her Collected Poems (*Samlede Digte*, 1998), two plays, children's books, an opera libretto, as well as countless articles, reviews, and translations. Her numerous prizes include: The Nordic Prize of the Swedish Academy, The Austrian State Prize for Literature, and Grand Prix des Biennales Internatio-nales de Poesie. Christensen died in January of this year.

A master of form, Christensen used elegant and com-plex formal structures that intensify her work's content. Her approach to form was in keeping with her conviction that literature is "a game, maybe even a tragic game—the game we play with a world that plays its own game with us." In *Azorno*, she magnified the game of fiction, with her narrative strategy of a novel within a novel within a novel.

Azorno resembles a house of mirrors. Images and passages recur with slight variations. The setting shifts between Copenhagen, Zurich, and Paris; points of view also shift, leaving the reader to puzzle out which of the characters is speaking. There are five women and two men. One man is a writer named Sampel, the other is Azorno, the main character of his novel. All the women are pregnant by Sampel. Some know each other, and they meet and write letters that comprise their novel about five women and a man named Sampel, who sometimes calls himself Azorno, and who is also writing a novel that may include one or more of the women.

The following excerpt, taken from a point about mid-way in the novel, returns to a previous setting, with a new narrator, Randi. Images and actions are repeated from earlier passages, but with significant differences. For example, the entire scene of Randi making a salad is repeated, almost verbatim, except this time, the salad ingredients include hemlock and rank lettuce opium. Whether or not the poisoning is "real" or fiction is unclear; shortly afterward, however, Randi is accused of murder by Louise, who's being held involuntarily, and the two have a scuffle in the same hospital room, with the same black button and nurses that appear later in the novel when Xenia, a different narrator, visits Sampel.

As the novel progresses, more and more questions arise: Has someone been killed? Is someone insane? Is someone held captive? Are some of the characters fabricating others? Is the whole story part of the novelist's book? Uncertainty reigns, further complicating the translator's job of keeping the various narrative strands straight, as they continue to multiply and intertwine with every page.

In this excerpt, Christensen compares a type of language usage to circus feats, concluding that "these tricks should be so strenuous that every word has to be in its place, and stretched to its outermost limit." This is a perfect description of her own writing, and perhaps gives some sense of the precariousness, as well as the extreme pleasure, of translating Christensen's masterwork.

Original text: Inger Christensen, *Azorno*.
Copenhagen: Gyldendal, 1967.

Azorno

Springvandet plaskede. Plurede. Strålen, der rejste sig fra midten af den lille cirkelformede kumme, steg og faldt i ét, steg op som gennem en plantestængel der længe har tørstet, krængede straks over i åben blomstring og faldt igen, blad efter blad, dryssede ned og knustes.

Eller steg som et sejt glasrør, der sendes lodret I vejret fra den liggende glaspusters mund, på toppen af hans kraft skummer over som en krave og glider direkte ud i et brusende skørt, uden nogen sinde at slynges bort som arme I heftig bevægelse, uden dans.

Eller steg. Og faldt. Som grønne planter grønne hår. Lange hår. Som langt hår i et fuldstændig frit fald ned gennem rummet. Dog aldrig fuldstndig frit. Altid let klæbet. Som hår der smyger sig om blodet. Der stiger. Steg-Og falder. Faldt.

Eller plaskede. Pludrede. Lagde sig ind til sit udspring og mumlede om og om igen på det første ord det havde lært.

Eller sang i den milde aftenluft.

I den lukkede gård.

Hvor jeg sad på den lave stenbænk i søjlegangen og døsede. Lyttede. Ønskede at jeg således kunne pludre og mumle på et sprog jeg ikke kendte, ikke forstod, og ikke skulle bruge til at indkredse og bestemme mine handlinger med. Mine næste handlinger. Ønskede at sproget skulle lade mig være i fred, holde tre skridts afstand og dér, midt på, fremføre sine kunster, jonglere, spise blår, danse og musicere, synge og balancere på de brogede bolde og frem for alt oprejse de selvsikkert svajende akrobatiske pyramider.

Og disse kunster skulle være så anstrengende, at hvert ord matte være på sin plads og til det yderste anspændt. . . .

Azorno

The fountain splashed. Babbled. The jet of water in the middle of the circular fountain rose and fell in one motion, rose up as through a plant stem that has long been thirsty, then immediately turned into an open flower and fell again, petal after petal, sprinkling down and shattering.

Or it rose like a resistant glass tube sent vertically into the air from the reclining glass blower's mouth, at the peak of his strength foaming like a collar that glides out to form a full skirt, without ever being flung like arms in a swift gesture, without ever dancing.

Or rose. And fell. Like green plants' green hair. Long hair. Like long hair in a completely free fall down through space. Although, never completely freely. Always a little sticky. Like hair that clings to the skin, that clings to the body, that clings to the blood. That rises. Rose. And falls. Fell.

Or splashed. Babbled. Settling on its source and mumbling over and over the first word it has learned.

Or sang in the mild evening air.

In the enclosed courtyard.

Where I sat on the low stone bench in the colonnade and dozed. Listened. Wished that I could in the same way babble and mumble in a language I didn't know or understand, and was not going to use to pin down and determine my actions. My next actions. Wished not to act. Wished to doze in the language, letting it spout like a fountain where opposing sources stream from all sides, rising and spouting forth. Wished that the language would leave me in peace, keeping three steps behind, and there, right in the middle, present its tricks, juggling, fire breathing, dancing, making music, singing, and balancing on multicolored balls and, above all, self-assuredly raising itself as swaying acrobatic pyramids.

And these tricks should be so strenuous that every word has to be in its place, and stretched to its outermost limit. A language that functions perfectly without my help, intervention. I wished for this. To buy time. To prevent a rash decision. Dozing.

Jumped up when the phone rang. Ready to run and get it. Ran for it. But didn't dare pick it up. Let it ring seven times while I slowly walked back and sat down on the stone bench. The fountain splashed. Overwhelmingly. Insisting loudly. Buzzing in my ears. Now sorry about my hesitation. A failure I regret. Sitting on the stone bench actually needing to confide in someone.

I saw that a little water mixed with dirt had seeped in under the door that connects the enclosed courtyard with the garden. It was as though a bleeding man were lying on the path out there, most likely across the path with his head under the wide rhubarb leaves.

Splashed. Buzzing in my ears.

I went and shut off the tap. The jets of water sank down. The surface of the water became calm and that dark metallic mouth became visible in the basin. In that slimy basin. Like a gun. Sent vertically into the air from the reclining glass blower's mouth. The assassin's hand.

I could hear the rain out in the garden. I lit a cigarette and leaned against the wall next to the sandstone sculpture. The little manikin swayed a bit. I took it by the arm and blew smoke over its lifeless eyes. A snail that had been sitting in the frizzy beard rolled down onto the tiles and landed the wrong side up. The puddle by the door had grown larger and was now the same dark color as the metallic nozzle in the middle of the basin.

I thought I might be freezing.

When the phone rang again, I threw the sculpture down and leaped so as not to trip over it, took the wide stone stairs two at a time with the help of a kind of climbing grip carved into the banister.

Yes, I said, out of breath. Yes. Yes. The operator gave me different bits of information. I was about to say yes, and stubbed out my cigarette on the wall. It left a black mark on the whitewash.

Yes, this is Randi, I said, and repeated it until I was sure I knew to whom I was speaking. Later I realized how unwise it was to reveal my name without knowing who it was, maybe a dangerous enemy. But I said yes, and said it again immediately, yes, yes this is Randi, yes.

The black cigarette mark on the whitewash was right by an old portrait, or more precisely, right by the nose of an unknown man in profile who was drawn on the dull paper with such a thin and black line, then framed and hung on the wall here in the gallery. At one time. I called him the composer. His kind expression was directly aimed at the mark. He always had his place here over the dark oak chest with a squared recess carved in the curved lid as if for the phone to fit. Some time ago. Later, the paper became dull, the oak dark, and the telephone was put in, although, there was never much light in the gallery. There isn't now either. Here you could comfortably forget who you were talking to and focus only on the composer, his eyes, his mouth. Hear his music.

Yes, I'm comfortable, I said, and sat up on the chest with my feet pressed against the row of rosettes that lined the lid.

And then Katarina told me all about Louise.

It grew into a very long, and actually, a very sad story, which I'm completely incapable of retelling, mainly because I object to Katarina's way of presenting it. She didn't speak about Louise, but about Louise's character.

The sunset had ended somewhere far beyond the rain and mountains. By the way, I don't think Katarina was even trying to get close to the truth, if once again just for a moment, I consider the truth to be the actual circumstances.

The end of the story was the frightening revelation that the story itself was precisely the reason for my being asked to drive as quickly as possible up through Germany, because Katarina, on account of this whole story, etc., needed me, etc., etc. It was said in three minutes. Do you want to know more? she asked.

—Yes, I said. What do you mean? I asked.

—Well, said Katarina, I wanted to ask you to rescue Louise.

—What do you mean? I said, sounding more foolish than before.

—Well, said Katarina, you have to help her understand that she's caught in a daydream.

—How could that be? I said helplessly.

—Well, said Katarina, you must explain everything to her, tell her that I was with Sampel the other day, and that he told me I'm the woman whom the main character in his novel meets on page eight.

What do you mean, I almost said, but stopped myself.

—And do you know who the main character is, the man? continued Katarina. It's Azorno.

—But what, I asked, what do you want me to do?

—Well, there's a lot to do, said Katarina. They've locked her up.

—How? I said.

—She's been hospitalized.

—Yes.

—She's being held involuntarily.

—Yes. I mean, yes.

—And she keeps mentioning you again and again.

—Does she? Why?

—Randi, she says, I'll never forget Randi, even though they're keeping her locked up.

—Keeping me locked up, I said.

Katarina said that Louise, from her confinement, tried to rescue me time after time from my confinement.

I said that I would try to reciprocate and as quickly as possible drive up through Germany.

Outside the rain beat with another tone. I packed. Most of it was already in the suitcase from last time. At the bottom were the finished sections of the novel with related used and unused notes. On top was a multicolored heap of extra bras, girdles, panties, stockings, sandals, scarves, gloves, creams, cosmetics, and a white hat, all rolled up in a glossy transparent plastic tube with a handle made of twisted gold thread. In a little mesh bag two blouses and one dress were crumpled together and yet, even in this condition they were ready to use because they were made of artificial fabric. I filled the holes and spaces in between with writing pads of different sizes, until I more or less had a flat surface of about five centimeters under the lid of the suitcase. On this flat part I put the unfinished sections of the novel with its related used and unused notes.

Then I started the car and drove slowly through the increasingly populated areas of Uetliberg, where the rain had stopped and the trees shone in the headlights, making my way onto broader and longer roads, where the rain had stopped and the asphalt shone in the headlights, and finally I let myself be pulled with the current into the city, where the rain . . . where the city lights were on.

The city glided by and settled behind my car that glided on and adjusted itself to the road that was now completely straight and sang in the mild evening air. Houses glided by, but mostly flat wide fields glided by, transforming themselves far out in the semidarkness into mountains where the rain had presumably also stopped and the invisible shone in the headlights. I rolled down the window and sang in the mild evening air.

It was a question of a release. Having to solve a problem, especially a problem related to a confinement, was an immediate relief to me. I breathed easier being forced to breathe in order to move, in order to solve a problem, especially a problem related to a confinement of another person, in this case, one of my friends, a woman no less, and, in this case, the woman I, on top of everything, had chosen to be the first person narrator of my novel, Louise, Via Napoli 3, but who was unfortunately confined and therefore replaced by Katarina, Katarina, Helgolands Street, who, in the meantime, had completely committed herself so fervently to Louise's release, that she, on top of everything, had asked me to drive as fast as possible up through Germany to help, which subsequently I did, am doing, even though at the same time, I had to become my own narrator in my own novel because of Louise's and Katarina's indisposition.

It was a question of gentleness. Solving something for others that cannot be solved for yourself demands first and foremost that you refrain from using all sharp objects, which no one wants to be cut with anyway. The problem therefore can be solved in two ways: with poison or freedom. Both equally gently. Every confinement can terminate from within: e.g. by giving the tree poison and quickly paralyzing the tissues in their multiple functions. When everything stands still in this way, a mute block, all movement begins to go downward: flowers disintegrate, leaves curl up, rustle, are carried away, twigs on branches dry up, break, and the trunk cracks, caves in. Slowly consumed by everything. Or the confinement can end from without: e.g. by giving the tree freedom, an excess of space, light, air, water, nourishment, by which it's made to unfold in a series of ecstatic flowerings, abruptly followed by exhaustion, withering. At last the tree dries up, a mute block that is slowly consumed by itself. By everything.

It was a question of an escape from reality. The problem that should have been solved was solved instead of the problem that should have been solved in the first place, and so on.

I sang in the mild evening air instead of writing a note for my novel about how in this place I might possibly sing in the mild evening air.

Everything in order to buy time.

As usual, I wished to sneak up on life, see how it was, and then make up my mind about whether I would live or not.

After we'd just been married, on our wedding night, I sneaked through the gallery to the bathroom in order to see him and make a decision.

When he went out, I sneaked down into the enclosed courtyard in the colonnade to see what he took with him, if he brought an umbrella and suitcase, a hat, glasses, gloves, card, cigarettes, maps, newspapers, flowers, chocolate, wine, boxes of underwear, perfume, if he took the car or not, and if he looked extroverted or introverted.

Or I sneaked from the enclosed courtyard into the garden in order to look through the hedges to see which way he drove, or perhaps walked, or ran, and if he looked back.

Or sneaked over to the window in the evening when he came home to see if he was alone.

Or sneaked over to the chair near the kitchen door to listen to him using the phone. Sneaked back and forth outside his door while he worked. Sneaked in and looked at him from behind and from the side. Sneaked into his wardrobe to see his face when he picked out his clothes. Sneaked in to see him looking at himself in the mirror. Sneaked in to sneak into his bed to see him get up. Lay and listened. Dozed. Heard him sneaking around. On the stone steps, on the terrace, by the door, on the tiled floor, in the drawing room, in room after room, in the dining room, in the living room, in the sitting room, in the garden room, in the salon, in the tea salon, the smoking salon, the literary salon, in the library and back again, in the salons, in the rooms, on the tiled floor. I heard the way he opened one of the umbrellas and let it twirl through his fingers, as he loved to do when he talked to the cat. The cat, by the way, that he once scolded for knocking over the large bouquet of multicolored tulips that he himself had just knocked over with the umbrella while he spoke about the imagery of certain artists, about water and water lilies, parasols and white clouds and fabrics, a wealth of the kind of luminous tangible things that are supposed to evoke the intangible and which now had suddenly assembled in one specific place in the world, resting around me like a bell, while I lay and listened to his sneaky steps. Dozing.

I could clearly hear that someone was coming. On the stone steps. It was she. On the terrace. Near the door. On the tiled floor. She had her own key. Was already standing near the door to the drawing room. And now moving through room after room. Dining room, living room, sitting room. And so she was already in the garden room before he ever got past the tiled floor at the foot of the stairs. He hurried through room after room. She, in the salon. He, in the dining room. She, in the tea salon. He, in the drawing room, sitting room. She, in the smoking salon. He, in the garden room. She, in the literary salon. He, in the salon. She, in the library and back again. He, in the tea salon, smoking salon, she, in the literary salon, smoking salon, he and she in the tea salon, he and she, he and she no longer sneaked any more, but danced together, ran, in fact, laughing through the salon, the garden room, the sitting room, the drawing room, talking, through the dining room, on the tiled floor, on the stairs, through the gallery, the wardrobe, past the mirror in his bedroom where the key was turned. I sneaked back and forth outside the door until at last they got tired and fell asleep

After that I sneaked around as though in a daze. It was a question of gentleness, by which I, with great determination, tried to decide whether he should have his freedom or a more insidious poison.

One day while I was dozing under the wide rhubarb leaves I looked from the garden through the hedge out on the street and suddenly saw her over there sneaking back and forth, and I felt like a diver who finds himself on the bottom of the ocean one minute and on solid ground the next, unable to hear whether the others are saying he's alive or dead, the air was so thick and warm and green and poisonous, because she had surely already discovered me and, with the greatest silence, sprayed her poison at me, a poison that quickly stripped all the leaf-flesh off my body, exposing my ribs, fluids, and reproductive system, causing me to cave in, collapse, crumble, almost vanish; yes, there was only a little dust remaining under the wide rhubarb leaves when I got up and sneaked into the house in order to buy more time.

At last, one evening, he sat in the kitchen at the large table with red-checked cloth waiting for his meal.

I took out a salad left over from the previous day. The greens had turned brown at the edges and had yellowish spots and creases, and the tomatoes were exceptionally pale.

I opened a can of asparagus and a can of shrimp, drained the liquid, and added them to the salad.

Then I stood there awhile tossing it as if in a daze.

I chopped an onion, some tomatoes, and a couple of hard-boiled eggs, whose whites were blue or violet or almost black, and threw it all into the salad bowl.

The original salad was now nearly hidden. I gave it a little toss, spread out my arms and almost laughed.

I then took out another bowl, made of ceramic and glazed in two shades of brown that flowed into each other in a speckled pattern. I poured in plenty of oil, shook in a good amount of wine vinegar, sprinkled in some salt and pepper and crushed a couple of garlic cloves.

Then I took the bowl in my arms, stirring and continuing the motion as in a dance across the wide floor.

I snipped a head of lettuce into strips, letting them fall into the dressing with some of the chopped hollow stems of the spotted hemlock, water hemlock, and the fine-toothed leaves of the rank lettuce opium, whose milky exudate quickly blended with the dressing. I poured the contents of the first bowl over the top and mixed it all together. And, as usual, I placed it with bread and wine on the red-checked cloth on the large kitchen table where he sat waiting for his meal.

Even after I had rolled down the window and sung in the mild evening air, I couldn't remember if I buried him under the wide rhubarb leaves, under the tiles near the fountain, under the sandstone sculpture, or if I placed him stiff and upright in one of the hollow columns in the colonnade in the enclosed courtyard, or lay him just as stiffly but horizontally in one of the many carved wooden chests along the wall of the gallery, for example, the one with the telephone under the picture of the composer continuously staring at the black spot on the whitewash where I stubbed out my cigarette while he listened to his own music. And dozed.

When I finally reached Louise, she sat there completely still, a mute block that was about to slowly consume itself. She was clearly pregnant.

The floor and walls of the hospital room were covered with yellow and blue tiles and, because of their intricate pattern, they shimmered with a greenish tint, a color intensified by the light entering the room, which wasn't direct sunlight but reflections from the apple orchard outside. There was a vase with a couple of tulips next to the bed. I had just bought a large bouquet of multicolored tulips at the entrance to the hospital grounds, but when Louise acted as though she didn't see me I put them down on the floor and sat on a wooden stool back by the door and stared at the picture hanging on the whitewashed portion of the wall over the tiles, and at the little black button that was used to call the staff. Katarina was sitting on the bed trying to get Louise to answer a variety of simple questions, but she was keeping her silence and her blank stare. Now and then I looked at Katarina from the side and after she lifted her arms a couple of times and her dress tightened, I became more and more certain that she was also pregnant.

Finally, Katarina got Louise to talk about mountain passes. They talked for a long time going back and forth about whether Passo S. Gottardo was 2109 or 2111, Sustenpass 2224 or 2222, Oberalppass 2044 or 2045 or 2046 and Passo del Lucomagno 1917, 1918, or 1919. Numbers and passes continued to buzz peacefully around a long line of place names—Tessin, Lugano, Bellinzona—Biasca, Lugano, Bellinzona—Lucerne, Zug, Biasca—Lucerne, Como, Chiasso—Chiasso, Biasca, Zug—Tessin, Biasca, Chiasso—making Louise more open and warm, but at the same time, tiring her out, for she suddenly said:

—She killed him.

They both looked at me, and Louise said point-blank:

—You've killed him.

Then she jumped up and began tearing at my clothes and hitting my face. I shoved her onto the bed and pressed the black button, and while Katarina and two nurses in blue who'd come hurrying in held her down, I thought about how it was all beginning to go badly for the novel I was writing, which was still in my suitcase, its finished and unfinished sections, with a layer in between consisting of extra bras, girdles, panties, stockings, sandals, scarves, gloves, creams, cosmetics, and a white hat, all rolled up in a glossy transparent plastic tube with a handle made of twisted gold thread.

For an Older Poet

Tomas Venclova | Translated by Ellen Hinsey from Lithuanian (Lithuania)

"For an Older Poet" is a free-verse poem, composed in four stanzas, which explores the relationship of the Lithuanian poet Tomas Venclova and his father, Antanas Venclova (1906–1971), a Lithuanian Soviet poet and chairman of the Lithuanian Writer's Union, among other activities. It is also a poem, as Tomas Venclova has noted, about "a generation of writers." In the wake of the break-up of the old empires following World War I, as well as the rise of German fascism and the onset of World War II, many writers struggled first-hand with the implications of national sovereignty, democracy, socialism, and communism. In the '30s, like many of his contemporaries, Tomas's father was drawn to communism and remained dedicated to its cause throughout his life. As Venclova has written:

> My father's fate was typical for a radical Eastern European writer: one may find similar biographies also in France, Spain, United States and elsewhere. In pre-war Lithuania, he edited an avant-garde literary magazine—perhaps the most lively one in the country—promoting Expressionism and Dadaism, as well as Walt Whitman, Upton Sinclair, and Romain Rolland. Since the magazine soon started to exhibit pro-Communist tendencies, it was closed by the Lithuanian censorship after the fifth issue. In 1940, my father became People's Commissar of Education of

the Sovietized Lithuania. He served as a war correspondent in World War II, and later was a well-known Soviet author, involved in various compromises characteristic for that era.

In 1956, as Tomas Venclova came of age, there would be increasing alienation between father and son. Already skeptical of the Soviet system, the poet became radicalized following the Soviet invasion of Hungary, an event of critical import for his generation, which regarded it as paradigmatic of Moscow's authentic motivations. In his late thirties, Tomas Venclova became involved with the Lithuanian and Soviet dissident movements, and was one of the five founding members of the Lithuanian Helsinki Group. Like other similar groups formed following the signing of the Helsinki Accords in 1975 with its famous Article 7 that promised respect for human rights, the Lithuanian Helsinki group would play its role in the eventual erosion of the Soviet system.

However, "For an Older Poet" is only in part about the impact of such events on the relationship between father and son. Written by a poet in the mature years of his life, the poem is also about the inevitability of human failings, about self-deception, and about the struggle for forgiveness, which, as Hannah Arendt has written, is the only thing that has the power to free us from the past, and to allow us to begin anew. Thus the poem explores with humility not only the divergent paths taken by a believing father and a dissident son, but also the sources of their affinities, of "language which had chosen" them both, about how Venclova's father's voice and cadence "resurfaces" in the poet's "foreign speech." For Venclova's memories of his father are complex, a complexity found as well in other European writers:

> Still, his private literary tastes were far from being Stalinist: it was he who acquainted me with Charles Baudelaire and Boris Pasternak, and gave me my first lessons in poetic technique. The "older poet" about whom I speak is far from being an exact portrait of my father. Although in the poem I have permitted myself some personal recollections, the poet represents his entire generation—and not just in Lithuania, but in other countries as well: one might think here about Ilya Ehrenburg, Louis Aragon and similar figures.

Through the labyrinths of memory and dream the poet leads the reader through the tight spaces of historical conflict and emotional complexity, to where, in an antiheroic moment of human truth, he does not, like Theseus, slay the dreaded Minotaur, but rather knows that one day son and father will stand beside each other "estranged and identical" in that painful paradox of flesh and blood that we call kinship.

Original text: Tomas Venclova, *Sankirta*. Vilnius: Lietuvos rašytojų sąjungos leidykla, 2005.

Vyresniam Poetui

Balkone tirpo sniegas. Elektra po apspurusiu šilko gaubtu
bloškė šešėlius ant sienų. Vienas jų siekė
statulą, kiti, nuklydę priešingon pusėn, mėgino
pažvelgti pro langą. "Štai šičia—dvi geros eilutės".
Tatai mudu jungė. Šiaip viską regėjom skirtingai:
gluosnį svyruoklį prie mūro, rausvų akmenų terasas,
putų mezginį vasaros smėlyje. Taip, atrandu savyje
tavo pagarbą ritmui, beformės medžiagos baimę,
bet atmenu tai, ko netrokštu atminti: kaip nuolat didėjo
atstumas tarp mūsų—netgi tada, kai drauge
sukom ratus apie stingstantį skverą; ir netgi tada,
kai sėdėjom žolėj prie Naručio, atlošę
galvas į dangų, stebėdami, kaip
sudriskęs žemėlapis plazda ir sklaidos aukštybėj.

For an Older Poet

Snow melted on the balcony. Electric light under the frayed silk shade
cast shadows on the walls. One of them touched
the statue—others, reaching in the opposite direction, tried
to peer out the window. "Right there—two good lines."
That's what brought us together. The rest we saw differently:
the weeping willow by the brick wall, terraces of ruddy stones,
summer sand's edge of foam. Yes, I discover within myself
your respect for rhythm, your distrust of formless content.
But I also remember what I wish I didn't: how the distance
between us constantly grew—even while we two
paced out circles around the cold park; even while
we sat in the grass by Naroch Lake, our heads
turned upward, watching how the torn
cartography of clouds unfurls and disintegrates up above.

Tai nebuvo lengva. Maždaug nuo penkiolikos metų
suvokiau tavo silpnybes, kurių nejutai
ar netgi jomis didžiavaisi. Pirmiausia dėl to
mokiaus alsuoti retėjančiu oru, keliauti
kėbule, žiebti degtuką lietuj,
gamintis varganą kavą, jausti panieką sau—
tai tarytum laidavo, jog mudu nebūsim panašūs
balsu ir braižu. Vis vien žinojai daugiau už mane:
apie žemę anapus pasienio stulpų, apie erą, kuri apibrėžė
mūsų poelgius tarsi akiratis; gal apie mirtį (nes víena kartà
buvai arčiau prie mirties); taip pat apie kalbą,
išsirinkusią mudu abu. Apie skiemenį, prielinksnį, kirtį.
Ir šiandien girdžiu, kaip tari: "Šlaitai? Turi būti: šlaitai",
lyg nuo to priklausytų išganymas. Gal ir priklausė.

Kartojai: "Kada manęs nebebus", ir tuo netikėjai.
Kaip visi, bijojai pranykti. Kaip daugelis, vyleis,
Kad knygos užtikrina bent antraeilį
nemirtingumą. Galbūt supratai, jog išduoda ir jos,
kai buvo jau kiek per vėlu. Nesipriešinai savo laikui.

It wasn't easy. When I was nearly fifteen,
I spied out your weaknesses, the ones you didn't want to own,
or even those of which you were proud. Because of this,
I learned to breathe thin Alpine air, to travel
on the backs of trucks, to light matches in the rain,
to brew bad coffee, to subject myself to self-scrutiny—
all of which, in a way, guaranteed we wouldn't be the same
in voice or script. Nevertheless, you knew more than me:
about the territory beyond the frontier's posts, about the era that circumscribed
our actions like a horizon line; perhaps, even about death (you were
a generation closer), and about language,
which had chosen us both. About syllables, prepositions, stress.
Even today I hear you say: "fáraway? It must be: farawáy,"
as if one's salvation depended on it. But then, perhaps it does.

You would repeat "When I'm no longer around," but you didn't believe it.
Like everyone, you were afraid to disappear. Like others, you hoped
books could at least guarantee a second-rate
immortality. Perhaps you realized that even books could betray you—
when it was too late. You didn't oppose your times.

("Ar galima kaltinti tą, kas vairuoja mašiną,
paklusdamas eismo signalams?") Žinoma, buvo dienų,
kurias bandei išbraukti iš sąmonės. Buvo bičiulių
už spygliuotų vielų. Kai kuriems padėjai—sakei, kad nevisad
tiems, kas atsimena gera. Gyvenai kaip kiti bendraamžiai,
nebent vientisiau—kad be garso krutinčiau lūpas
ir kartočiau žodžius, kuriais nebuvai palydėtas:
amžiną atilsį, Viešpatie, duoki jiems. Be slogučių.
Ir Amžinoji Šviesa jiems tešviečia. Kaip šachtos lempelė.

Pastaruoju metu retai sapnuoju tave,
bet kartais sapnuoju. Abudu skubam stotin,
klumpam, nespėjam. Esu perone, traukinys
išeis po minutės. Turiu tave susirasti,
bet žinau, kad nerasiu—gaišuoji, sunkus lagaminas,
koridoriai painūs ir laiptų per daug. Tebesi,
kol seku tavo eigasties aidą, netolygų alsavimą, skausmą
už krūtinkaulio (jį kada ne kada patiriu pats). Tavo gestai gyvi
                                                        manyje,
kad ir kiek besipriešinčiau. Tavo šnekos intervalai

"How can you blame someone who, at the wheel of his car—
follows the traffic rules?" Of course, there were days
you wished to strike from your consciousness. There were friends
behind barbed wire. You helped some of them—said they
didn't remember the good you'd done. You lived like your contemporaries,
perhaps more consistently—so that I might noiselessly move my lips
repeating the words not said after your departure:
may they rest in peace, Lord. Without nightmares.
And may Eternal Light shine upon them. Like a light in a coal mine.

You rarely appear in dreams these days,
but sometimes you do. We are both hurrying to the station,
stumbling, running late. I stand on the platform, the train
will pull out any second. I must find you,
but I know I won't be able—you are delayed somewhere, the suitcase is heavy,
the corridors are labyrinthine, there are too many steps. But you live on
as long as I follow the echo of your footsteps, your unsteady breathing, the pain
in your chest (which I sometimes also feel). Your gestures continue in me,
no matter how hard I try to suppress them. The cadence of your voice
resurfaces in my foreign speech. As you diminish,

atsiliepia mano skirtingoj šnekoj. Kada sumažėja
tavęs, mažėju ir aš. Vieną sykį nubusiu stoty
ir tave pamatysiu. Žibintas vagono gale
sukrutės ir nutols—greičiau ir greičiau,—o mudu stovėsim,
nežiūrėdami vienas į kitą, svetimi ir tapatūs.

I also grow smaller. One day I'll wake up in the station
and see you. The lamp suspended from the carriage's end
will sway and start to pull away—pick up speed—but we'll remain standing,
without looking at each other, estranged and identical.

Cities Without Palms

Tarek Eltayeb | Translated by Kareem James Abu-Zeid from Arabic (Sudan)

The son of Sudanese parents, Tarek Eltayeb was born in Cairo in 1959, where he lived until moving to Vienna in 1984. He took on many jobs in order to finance his studies in Austria, including selling newspapers and washing dishes. He is now a professor of International Management in Krems, Austria, and has earned fame as both a poet and a novelist in the Arab-speaking world.

Tarek's early experiences in Europe greatly inform his writing, much of which deals with the experience of immigrants (both documented and undocumented) in modern European societies. Indeed, one of the leitmotifs of Tarek's writing as a whole is the insistent feeling of *ghurba*, an Arabic word that has no exact equivalent in the English language, though estrangement, alienation, and homesickness are all approximations. *Ghurba* is the feeling of strangeness (and often longing) that one has in a foreign land, far from one's homeland.

Yet in Tarek's work, the term *ghurba* is not a temporary emotional state that can be discarded, but rather a more permanent existential condition. This is certainly true of Tarek's first novel, *Cities Without Palms*, which he completed in 1988, and from which the following four excerpts come. In this powerful work, Hamza, the novel's narrator, has no choice but to set out alone from his native village and seek work in the city, in a desperate attempt to support his mother and sisters and save them from the famine and disease that are sweeping across the Sudanese countryside. Hamza travels from Sudan to Egypt, and then onwards to Europe, constantly struggling against poverty, xenophobia, and that *ghurba* that he has been forced to take on as a mode of life.

Although I had translated quite a bit of Arabic poetry in the past, *Cities Without Palms* was the first full novel that I have ever worked on. At first, I must confess to being remarkably overwhelmed by the sheer number of words that suddenly confronted me: the intense linguistic paucity of poetry had suddenly been replaced with a very daunting verbal mass. But the challenge was an exciting one, and was made much easier by the fact that I no longer had to worry about capturing meter or rhyme. The question of *tone*, however, suddenly took on immense importance.

Hamza's first-person narrative is simple yet elegant, though not exactly straightforward: Hamza is on a certain level an extremely naive narrator, and thus Tarek takes care not to endow him with too much flowery language or too many complex Arabic linguistic structures, as this would undermine the credibility of his character. Yet neither is the tone of the novel a colloquial one: the novel is still written in very literary Arabic, and Tarek makes no use of the Arabic dialects, not even in the novel's many dialogues. Walking this fine line—capturing both the narrative's relative simplicity as well as its unmistakable literary quality—was undoubtedly the greatest difficulty that I faced in translating *Cities Without Palms*.

Original text: Tarek Eltayeb, *Mudun bila nakhil.*
Cairo: Al-Hadara Publishing, 1992.

مدن بلا نخيل

جالسا على حجر كبير أمام باب دارنا المبنية من الطين, ماسكا في يدي عودا يابسا, إلى طرف منه تسري أفكار كثيرة متزاحمة, وفي طرفه الآخر تعبث يدي بخطوط وحروف غريبة, فأرسم على الأرض حروفا وأشكالا ربما تعني ما لا أعني, فأنا غارق في أفكاري الحزينة.

أضغط بالعود اليابس على الأرض المتشققة الجدباء, في غل وغضب, وثورة عنيفة في داخلي تستقر مرارتها في حلقي, فأبصق على الأرض لاعنا هذا الفقر وهذا الجدب الذي حل بنا بلا رحمة, وأتنهد متذكرا أبي وما فعله بنا, فأبصق مرة أخرى. إني أكره كرها لا حد له, وأكيد أنه يكرهني ويكره أمي وأختيَّ الصغيرتين أيضا, وإلا فلماذا تركنا بعد أن تزوج من امرأة أخرى, ولم نسمع منه شيئا. مرة يقال لنا إنه في سوق الخرطوم يبيع المرطبات, ومرة يقال إنه يعمل في السكة الحديد بوادي حلفا, ومرة نسمع أنه ذهب إلى مصر حيث يعمل نادلا في أحد المقاهي.

لعنة على هذه الحياة بما فيها! إن لم يكن قادرا على

إعالة أسرة, فلماذا تزوج إذن, ثم لماذا تركنا وهرب.

يزداد ضغطي على العود اليابس, ينكسر عدة مرات حتى أجد أطراف أصابعي تلامس شقوق الأرض, أنظر إلى هذه الشقوق المتقاطعة كنسيج العنكبوت, وأحاول أن أخفيها, مزيحا بقدميَّ التراب بين شقوقها, لكن ماذا تفعل قدمان صغيرتان لقرية بأكملها, فمنذ أن زحف التصحر الجدب وعزت الأمطار, بدأت الويلات تأتينا بلا هوادة. جفاف ومرض, عذاب وموت, وما زلنا نحيا موتى ونموت أحياء. تهب ريح تحمل معها غبارا, فأرخي عينيَّ لحظات ثم أفتحهما لأرى قدميَّ السوداوين معفرتين بتراب ميت, تراب يرغب في أن يبتلعني حيا, كما ابتلع المئات من أهل قريتا, وأهل القرى المجاورة. أريد أن أبكي ولا أستطيع, أجاهد حتى تسقط قطرة دمع واحدة من عيني, فتأبى السقوط, كأني أنا أيضا أصبحت جافا خاويا تماما مثل قريتنا. ألعن أبي مرة أخرى, فقد علمني قبل أن يتركنا, أن البكاء للنساء فقط, وعلى الرجل ألا يبكي مهما حدث له. لعنة عليك أيها الحكيم الجبان! كان

Cities Without Palms

Sitting on a rock in front of our mud-brick house, I hold a dry stick in my hand. My many competing thoughts flow into one end of it, while its other end sketches strange lines and letters in the earth. If there is any meaning in these forms, it is unintended, for I am lost in my sad thoughts.

I press the stick down into the cracked, barren earth in anger and disgust. The violence and bitterness inside of me rises to my throat: I spit on the ground, cursing this merciless poverty and desolation. Then I sigh, remembering my father and what he did to us, and spit once more. I hate that man, and I am sure he hates me and my mother, and my two younger sisters as well. Why else would he marry another woman and abandon us like that? We never heard anything from him again, though we were once told that he was selling soda at a souk in Khartoum,

and once that he was working on the railroad at Wadi Halfa, and another time that he had gone to Egypt and was working as a waiter in a coffeehouse.

Curse this life. Why did he abandon us? If he was incapable of supporting a family, why did he get married in the first place?

I increase the pressure on the dried-out stick, breaking it repeatedly until my fingertips are touching the clefts in the ground. I look at these cracks that crisscross the earth like a cobweb and, using my feet, try to cover them up with dirt. But what can two small feet do for an entire village? The desert keeps growing, and sorrow, not rain, is all that comes to us. Drought and disease, agony and death: we are the dying, the living dead. A dusty wind blows in, so I close my eyes for a few moments, then open them to see my black feet covered in dead dust, dust that wants to swallow me alive just as it swallowed hundreds of people from our village, and many from the neighboring villages too. I want to cry, but I cannot. I try to force a single teardrop from my eye, but it refuses to fall, as if I too have become utterly dry and desolate, like our village. I curse my father once again. Before he left, he taught me that weeping was for women and that a man must never cry, no matter what the circumstances. Curse your wisdom, you coward. I wish you had kept it to yourself.

One of the palm fronds that forms the roof of our poor house flies off and falls to the ground. I pick it up between my fingertips. I think and spit, then think some more. I twist the frond around the tip of my ring finger and press down on it. I feel nothing, even as its sharp tip cuts into my skin. I press my finger into the dirt, just as we did when we were children. Whenever one of us hurt our foot or hand while playing, we simply pressed the wound into the earth until the bleeding stopped, and then we continued with our game.

I watch the children playing. Where are the ones today that resemble my childhood friends? I see only the specters of children, small ghosts dancing before me. Hunger has worn them down; bones protrude from their emaciated bodies; mangy, dust-colored skin covers their ribs and knees. Some of them are running around. Some of them are yelling. And others, too thin and weak to move, sit on the ground and take part in the game from a distance by screaming, only by screaming. This is a new game with which I am not familiar. When one of the children sees the others move away from him, he knows that they do not want him to join in the game, not even by shouting. This causes him to yell even more, and to keep yelling until his voice cracks. He weeps hoarsely until his mother comes and suckles him from breasts that resemble my mother's empty purse. I look at the child, and his two large, expectant eyes seem to cover his entire face. One of his hands clutches his mother's breast and the other her braids, and all the while flies gather around his eyes and pustules; they crowd around the wounds of his rickety body. Then they move to his mouth, hoping to share in his mother's milk; but nothing is there, so they return to assailing his emaciated body, falling upon its every wound—if there is no milk, then let there be blood.

Even if the entire village were to die, the flies would still remain. During the day they suck the children's blood, retreating only at night, when the mosquitoes come to claim their share. Their share of the remaining blood. . . .

❖

The warm summer permits me to sleep in the open air, and I spend the next nine nights in public parks. When I wake up each morning, I feel as if mites—borne on the winds I endure as I sleep—have been gnawing on my bones all night. I spend the days looking for work, walking all across the city until my sandals are almost worn away. On the tenth day I run out of money. I head toward the spice market and ask every person with a shop, cart, or stand about work, but they have nothing for me, not even when I tell them that I am willing to work for room and board alone. I stamp around in rage, spitting and swearing and asking shopkeeper after shopkeeper, but it is hopeless. I fear for my mother and sisters. I rub my amulet and ask its forgiveness. I look at the watch on my arm, wishing I could find Abd al-Malik: he would welcome me with open arms; he would manage to find me some work.

I hold onto a final vestige of hope, but it dies as the amulet fails to procure any work for me. In a loud voice, I curse the market and all its traders and spices; I curse the injustice and the demons of this world. I left my family under hunger's dominion, and came here to provide them with money for food. I was forced to steal, yet when I gave up theft to look for proper work I found that all paths to an honest living were blocked.

I will be forced to steal again, and this time I will not regret it: Theft is no crime for those who truly know hunger.

That night I make my way from the cinema to the *fuul* restaurant, and from there to the spice market, intending to steal some spices and sell them the next day. The shopkeepers do not fully close up their stores at night, and I think I can sneak in and out without any trouble, for no one sleeps in the *souk* and the whole place is empty at night. I have grown accustomed to stealing in the past two months, and this should not be too difficult for me.

I sneak into the *souk* carrying some paper bags. Night's dark robes provide ample cover—I cannot even see my hands in front of my face. Yet my many daytime visits here have taught me where each alley leads, where each shop is to be found.

I easily manage to open up the first shop. I grope among the sacks of spices in the darkness and tensely fill my bags in haste. One sack contains dried hibiscus, another fenugreek, another corn. I feel my way through them, placing my full bags by the door of the shop. I become greedy though, and as I look to fill up my very last bag, I unfortunately open a sack of chili powder. The powder fills my nostrils as I unwittingly scoop out a handful of the stuff, and I start to cough and sneeze as never before. I manage to muffle some of my sneezing, but not all of it.

I quickly pick up my bags and close the shop behind me, hurrying on my way, coughing and spitting as I run.

The *souk* is large, with many long alleyways. I hear the sound of footsteps coming toward me from the top of one of the alleys, so I hide by one of the stores and desperately try to stem the sneezing and coughing, but a few suppressed coughs still sneak out of me. I stare vainly into the darkness, then try to see with my ears.

Suddenly I hear someone sneezing from within the shop beside me. The sneezing worsens, and I am afraid that it might be coming from one of the shopkeepers. I set off again, running recklessly through the market like a terrified rabbit, no longer caring about whether I crash into someone, for fear can sometimes be a source of boldness.

The crisis is over at the end of the alley. My breathing is raspy from the chili, the fear, and the running, but I have finally reached the far end of the *souk*, and am now on the edge of one of the public parks where I had slept the past few days. I broke one of the lamps there so

I could sleep in peace, away from the prying eyes of the police and the biting mosquitoes. . . .

After much time and practice, I no longer cough or sneeze, nor do I run through the alleys of the *souk*, but rather proceed calmly about my business. I begin to make some money, and I also move from my spot in the park to the ruins of a shack behind the camel market that is only ever approached by stray dogs, or by some drunkard coming by to vomit or piss on one of the ramshackle walls. The smell is horrible here, but I have trained my nose well, and now it only smells what I want it to. . . .

❖

And so I arrive in Egypt, and set foot in this land of legend, this country Sheikh al-Faki had told me so much about. Who in our village would believe that I am here? Sheikh al-Faki himself would not believe it, and if he did find out he would probably go into shock, for he was the only explorer ever to venture out of the village, and he

would not be pleased with insignificant Hamza undertaking a voyage reserved for more prominent people.

These thoughts pass through my mind as I leave the border control area and head to the broad open area behind the port to look for a bathroom. I see the scattered silhouettes of people at the far end of the place. Some of them are standing up like lofty palms, and others are squatting. At first I think that they are praying, but then why wouldn't everyone be praying together? When I get closer I realize what they are doing and, picking a spot a little way from the others, follow their lead.

Feeling hungry, I head to a coffeehouse where men are sitting in small close-knit groups, most of them discussing business and arguing about money and wages. An elderly man is sitting at the front, his rickety chair held together with twine. There is an old desk with a single drawer in front of him, and a tray holding a cup of tea on top of the desk. One woman and a couple of men are standing there. He is changing money for them, taking their Sudanese dinars and giving them Egyptian pounds.

I sit down to order something to eat, but they have nothing but cookies here. I order a few of them, which fail to sate my hunger. The high prices keep me from ordering any more, however.

I stay there a while and watch the people as they talk in many different dialects, most of which I cannot understand. Then I fall asleep for a bit, my head resting on the small table in front of me. The waiter wakes me though, and puts another cup of tea in front of me. When I tell him that I did not order one, he replies: "You can't sit here for free."

It is eleven o'clock in the morning, but the train will not be coming until two in the afternoon. I sit up in my chair and sip my tea extremely slowly. The waiter watches the liquid sink in the cup, and as soon as it is empty he pounces on me with another one. I know I will have to pay for it, but I do not object. I sip the tea like a suckling child, trying to ignore the waiter. He hovers around me like a kite bird, singing some songs that I cannot fully understand, but that somehow seem to be mocking me, putting me ill at ease.

I leave the café a half-hour later, paying the bill on the way out. Now the waiter can finally have some peace from me, and I from him.

Time passes slowly. It keeps getting hotter, until there is nothing else to do but go back to the coffeehouse and order a bottle of cola from the waiter. It occurs to me that he looks a bit like a frog, though I am not sure what has left me with this impression—his obnoxious behavior, perhaps. He sees me and quickly makes some room for me to sit. I order my drink. He asks if I am hungry but I say no, so he quickly brings me the cola. Then the frog proceeds to stare fixedly at the bottle until the time comes to leap at me with another one, both of us enjoying this new game—"drink and jump"—together. Indeed, it seems to be the waiter's favorite pastime. Perhaps it is his physique that reminds me of a frog, or the way he springs from one table to another, bringing the customers more tea, cola and coffee even though they have not ordered any of it. It could also be his scheming eyes that pop out of their sockets just a little more than they should, or his hoarse and croaking voice. Or maybe it is all of this together.

I pass the time with this silent game, and drink three bottles of cola while laughing bitterly to myself. I leave around one in the afternoon. The frog croaks mockingly in my face as I go. . . .

❊

My first month in France ends, and with it my legal period of stay. Now, in my second month, I am illegal just like all the rest. I walk the streets like a rat, and whenever I see a police car or an officer's uniform I scurry into the first alley I can find, or rush into a shop at random—I ask for soap at the butcher's and for bread at a bookstore. I have heard about what happens when you get caught: I would be forced to spend the night in prison and would then be deported back to Sudan, while all my money sits in a bank here in France.

My fear and worry grow, and finally I go to the bank and withdraw all my money. Once back at the house, I go to the bathroom so that no one can see me and stitch the money to the inside of my trousers. The others are in dire straits. They have run out of money, and cannot even afford cigarettes anymore.

A few days later, the group decides to go to Holland. They have heard that the situation is better there than in France, and that there is work to be found. I decide to go with them and stick this thing out to the end.

Our main problem is that all our legal periods of stay here in France ended long ago, which means there is no chance of any of us obtaining an entry visa to Holland. But the most experienced man in our group, who has been all over Europe, says he has a way to get us across the border. He suggests that we travel together by train from Lyon to Paris, and from there to Amsterdam via Belgium.

The plan is for all of us to go hide in the train's bathrooms as it approaches the border, and to wait there until the border police have finished going through the train. He says he has traveled this way several times before. As the group listens to him, a look of sudden earnestness appears on their faces. The idea of this dangerous plan scares me, and I try not to show my fear. I look at the others' faces for reassurance, but fail to find any there.

We buy tickets to Paris, and from Paris to Brussels, so that we can stay on the same train until the border. We board the train, and my fear grows with each passing mile. I am drenched in sweat, and begin to wish that I had not undertaken this journey. But the hand of fate keeps pulling me on invisible strings toward danger, toward the unknown. I wish my mother would call me home, save me from this wrenching, wandering existence. I touch the amulet and seek its blessing.

I forget about everything else the moment we split up and head to separate cars of the train. Each of us hides in one of the bathrooms, and the train draws ever closer to the France-Belgium border.

I stay in the bathroom for exactly sixteen minutes, during which I look at my watch more than forty times. I almost come out to give myself up and have them send me away. I hear voices outside, and I know that they have figured out where we are hiding. They are coming after us, taking us out of the bathrooms one after the other. I look for a hole in the door so I can see what is happening, but I cannot find one. So I prick up my ears instead, though I cannot understand a word they are saying. I hold my breath and remain perfectly still.

Time passes, yet the train does not move. I can hear a police car entering the station. I stay nailed to the spot, cursing and swearing to myself. A few more minutes pass, and still I am waiting for the inevitable knock on the bathroom door, for them to take me away, submissive and defeated.

Mozart's Third Brain

Göran Sonnevi | Translated by Rika Lesser from Swedish (Sweden)

"Mozart's Third Brain" is the 190-page title poem from *Mozarts Tredje Hjärna*, Göran Sonnevi's thirteenth book of poems, which encompassed another ninety pages of discrete shorter poems called "Disparates," after Goya's etchings and aquatints. The title poem, written between 1992 and 1996, comprises 144 sections bearing roman numerals. Some of these appeared in previous volumes of TWO LINES (*Crossings*, 2000; *Bodies*, 2005). Yale University Press will publish the poem in its entirety, with my preface and notes and a foreword by Rosanna Warren, in fall 2009.

Describing Sonnevi's work, I often quote the cel-ebrated novelist Göran Tunström (1937–2000) concerning Sonnevi's attempt to write "a single long poem, a commentary on everything that comes within range of his language." In her foreword to *Mozart's Third Brain*, Rosanna Warren describes it thus: "Sonnevi reinvents the long poem, and reinvents poetic language. What threat-ens to sprawl, or to squander itself in random Op-Ed notations, turns out to engage in a disciplined quest to integrate private consciousness . . . into wider and wider connections between the natural world (rocks, plants, and weather); the emotional world of friendship, family, and erotic love; and the political realm." I characterize

Sonnevi's oeuvre as lyric, meditative, and visionary. I am conscious of seeking a timeless tonal quality in the voices of poets I choose to translate.

Section XCVIII is one of the few in which Mozart himself—his music, his image, his brain—arises. Were it not for the references to Schoenberg and to brain science, one would hardly know which century the poem came from, so basic and human are the express concerns: pain, violence, mercy, compassion, the one and the many, and the need not only for the sounds of music and speech, but also for the capacity to listen.

The printed page does not provide the distinctive sound of the poet's living voice, which was the music I needed to hear before I began to translate Sonnevi's work. He stutters when he speaks but not when he reads before an audience. We have always agreed on the overriding importance of speech rhythm in translation. I translate the poems so that he can comfortably read them aloud in English.

More than fifteen years have elapsed since my first selection of Sonnevi's poetry, *A Child Is Not a Knife* (Princeton, 1993), was published. Before then, the only separate edition of Sonnevi's work in English was a bilingual chapbook translated by Robert Bly: *The Economy Spinning Faster and Faster* (New York: Sun, 1982). It was not my intention to become Sonnevi's sole English-language translator, but it seems I have assumed that role since the mid-1980s. As his work and international reputation have grown and spread, it has been a great honor and a tremendous responsibility to remain virtually his sole English-language translator. Working on and with this poet for twenty-five years has become no less challenging. We continually argue over words and concepts in Swedish and English. We also laugh.

Original text: Göran Sonnevi,
Mozarts Tredje Hjärna. Stockholm: Bonniers, 1996.

Mozarts Tredje Hjärna

XCVIII

Öppningarna till det underbara genom musiken . . .   Som om jag varit
rädd för Paradis-aspekterna, länge   Tvärs genom musiken av
mörker   Alla dem som klingande värjer sina liv   Jag själv
tafatt del av denna musik   Som ändå strömmar ur min kropp
mina händer   Det klingande ropet   I stäven till Charons båt . . .

Mozarts hjärnas hemlighet säger tidskriftsrubriken under
porträttet av Mozartbarnet, med fingrarna på klaviaturen
Ansiktet är belyst snett framifrån, eller uppifrån   Skuggorna
stämmer inte   Han bär peruk, röd rock   Jag läser om den vänstra
tinninglobens rikare utveckling hos personer med absolut gehör
och undrar om det verkligen gäller Mozart . . .   Och att detta då
skulle ha samband med språket   Jag tänker på den exakta tonhöjdens
drift, förändring, sedan 1700-talet, nästan en halv ton . . .
Jag har lyssnat på Schönbergs stycke för orgel, dess vandring
allt djupare in i mysteriets labyrint, levande, dess bön . . .

Mozart's Third Brain

XCVIII

The openings to the marvelous through music . . .   As if I'd been
afraid of the Paradise aspects for a long time   Straight through the music of
darkness   All those who resoundingly defend their lives   I myself
an awkward part of this music   That nonetheless streams from my body,
my hands   The resounding cry   In the stem of Charon's boat . . .

The Secret of Mozart's Brain reads the title of an article under
a portrait of the child Mozart, his fingers on the keyboard
The face is illuminated obliquely from the front or from above   The shadows
aren't right   He wears a wig, a red jacket   I'm reading about the left
frontal lobe's richer development in those who have absolute pitch
and wonder whether this actually pertains to Mozart . . .   That this then
should be connected with language   I'm thinking about tonal drift,
the variation in exact pitch since the 1700s, almost a half tone . . .
I have listened to Schoenberg's work for the organ, its wandering
all the more deeply into the labyrinth of mystery, alive, its prayer . . .

Jag hör sluttonens avlagringar, dess djupa schakt in i tiden
vibrerande   Åter känner jag den djupa satisfactionen, fastän
detta stycke brukar avfärdas, som underligt, formlöst, en anomali . . .
Vi är det språk vi faktiskt talar; vi är i dess sång, oändlig

Det finns musik där tvivlet och smärtan sätts in på varje
ton, varje fragment av klang . . .   Som om just detta var
självklarhetens morgon, del av det mänskliga, i guds-
förhållandet . . .   Höra denna dynamik   Höra detta som bön, smärt-
bönen, där det aldrig finns några garantier   Spela så!

Som om Mozartklangen var nästan det enda
som inte brändes till aska av smärtklangen, i sina
vandrande serier . . .   Varje dag tafatta försök   Varje dag
det bländande våldets klang, i alla sina spegelvärldar
Jag rör mig i trafiken   Nästan alla människor rör sig
Du som berättar om sömnen, att du sover nästan hela tiden,
men att du tänker, hela tiden egna tankar, inte andras, om
våldet, narcissismen, virveln av uppväxande behov . . .
Ja, säger jag, och ger mig in i en historisk redogörelse
Jag undrar sedan över detta   Tiden klipper av samtalet

I hear the strata within the final note, its deep shaft into time,
vibrating   Again I feel deep satisfaction, although
this piece is usually dismissed as strange, formless, an anomaly . . .
We are the language we actually speak; we are in its endless song

There is music where doubt and pain come in on every
note, every fragment of sound . . .   As if just this were
the dawning of clarity, part of the human, in human relation
to God . . .   To hear this dynamic   To hear this as prayer, pain's
prayer, where there are never any guarantees   Play that way!

As if the sound of Mozart were almost the only one
not burnt to ash by the sound of pain, in its
wandering series . . .   Every day awkward attempts   Every day
the sound of blinding violence, in all its mirror-worlds
I move in traffic   Almost all people move
You who talk to me about sleep, telling me you sleep almost all the time,
but that you think, always think your own thoughts, not those of others, about
violence, narcissism, the vortex of rising need . . .
Yes, I say, and launch into a historical account
Later I wonder about this   Time cuts the conversation short

Den oerhörda sammanfattningen av många hjärnor . . .   I en
samhällelig form   Också för destruktionen   Den kollektive
Mozart rusande mot avgrunden, fallande, som Don Giovanni
Viva la libertà! I vilket universellt samhälle sker integrationen
där vetenskapen inte räcker   Därför att också den är avgrund
Krigets klyvnader öppnas överallt på nytt, som i en Helvetets
tafatthet . . .   Också de är alltför snabba formaliseringar
i det som är utan barmhärtighet, eller ens medkänsla   Helvetet
fanns inte före skapelsen   Och skall heller inte vara för evigt
Varje form är den sista   Som om detta var förintelsepunkten i
                                                                våra hjärnor . . .

Djärvheten fräckheten, som spräcker det existerande enda,
och människan som faller genom avgrundseonerna, i hierarkierna
av mörka speglar, också de bländande, med sitt mörker
Hur skall jag förklara för dig det ondas existens?
Varför det är vidrigt att slå, skada, döda en annan—

Under demoktratins hinna växer det totalitära, som ett generaliserat
sår   Kring alla väggarna tystnad   Mellan lagarna öppnar sig
ny potentialitet   Också ny smärta, nya sår   På nästan oändligt avstånd
dansen   Den som vi bär   Den som bär oss   Jag hörde dig, hör dig

The enormous summary of many brains . . .   In a
societal form   Also for destruction   The collective
Mozart rushing toward the abyss, falling, like Don Giovanni
Viva la libertà! In which universal society does integration occur,
where science is insufficient   Because it, too, is an abyss
The rifts of war open everywhere anew, as with Hellish
awkwardness . . .   These formalizations are also altogether too rapid
in what is without mercy, or even without compassion   Hell
did not exist before creation   Nor shall it last eternally
Every form is the last   As if this were the annihilation point in
                                                        our brains . . .

The boldness, the brashness, which bursts the existing One,
and the man who falls through abysses, through eons, in the hierarchies
of dark mirrors, these, too, blinding with their darkness
How shall I explain to you the existence of evil?
Why it is repulsive to strike, wound, kill someone else—

Beneath the membrane of democracy the totalitarian grows, like a generalized
sore   Around all the walls is silence   Between the laws
new potentiality opens   Also new pain, new wounds   At an almost infinite distance:
the dance   That we carry   That carries us   I heard you, hear you

The Man Who Tried to Go to Heaven

Rogelio Riverón | Translated by Elizabeth Bell from Spanish (Cuba)

In this short story, an old man's fancy turns to thoughts of death—but no ordinary transition to the beyond. His young subordinate recounts the bizarre expedition, and through his words we learn all we know of the old man, the only other character in the story, except for the absent birds.

Cuban author Rogelio Riverón has described some of his work as attempting to "mingle sarcastic, dramatic, humorous, and sensual tones," and this brief tale presents us with just such a multivalent voice. The narrator, a rural youth on the brink of manhood, tells the story in a register that fluctuates from slang to elevated expres-sion, with the main flow of his speech marking smaller vacillations in between. A translator seeking to force him into the mold of a traditional rustic character is doomed to fail or betray.

My difficulties with one phrase, which at first I found the most mysterious in the text, turned out to be rooted in my ignorance of Cuban custom. In many cultures one would soothe someone who was ill or injured by placing a cool cloth on the sufferer's brow; in Cuba the palliative is to sprinkle water on the person's neck. You don't get this from a dictionary. (Thanks to my informant and pal, poet Félix Lizárraga.)

"I write because it's practically the only thing I know how to do," says Rogelio Riverón.

When an interviewer pressed the issue with another "Why do you write?" query, Riverón said: "If I were older I might answer that I do it as a service to culture. For now, I'd chop one syllable off that embarrassing word and say I do it as a vice, or my fate."

Asked another, "What do you like to do besides write?"

The reply: "Write."

At forty-four, Riverón has won numerous prizes, including the 2008 Italo Calvino Award, granted by the National Union of Writers and Artists of Cuba in conjunction with the Italian cultural organization ARCI and the Grupo Fundativo Italo Calvino; and the 2007 Julio Cortázar Award for short stories. He is also a critic, journalist, anthologist, novelist, and poet, but remains deeply committed to the short story as a genre.

The two extraordinary protagonists in *The Man Who Tried to Go to Heaven* whet the curiosity. Are his characters in any sense alter egos?

Riverón: "I am capable of sitting down and coming up with a story like many writers. There's nothing exceptional about this. There's very little of the autobiographical. The characters don't have anything to do with me. It frightens me to think that the moment could come when I have to wait to live in order to write fiction."

Original Text: Rogelio Riverón, "El hombre que quería subir al cielo" from the collection *Subir al cielo y otras equivocaciones*. Havana: Editorial Letras, 1996.

El hombre que quería subir al cielo

. . . como lo son también los condenados a vagar por los grises parajes del Universo.

BORIS PASTERNAK

Todo le comenzó al cumplir los setenta. No imaginaba que un viejo de setenta años pudiera ser tan majadero, y no se me puede olvidar que por su culpa estoy como estoy. En cuanto empecé a despuntar, a crecer de verdad, me cayó del cielo un baldado. Por eso aunque no quisiera, a veces lo odio; lo odio realmente y cuando eso ocurre me digo para calmarme que él no tiene la culpa, al menos no toda, pero luego me vuelva bruto y pienso paralítico asqueroso, carcamal desalmado, mira cómo me has puesto. Habiendo podido morirte como todo el mundo, se te ocurrió sin embardo ponerte con tanta indecencia. Egoísta has sido

al no pensar en mí que te seguí por llanos y pantanos, por lomas y bosques para desembocar a esta tierra fría y extraña, tierra mil veces maldita que me pone los pelos de punta; tierra embrujada por la que deambulo, señero y pusilánime, en espera de la ocasión para abandonarla.

Fue el propio día de su cumpleaños. Esa mañana apenas comenzó a aclarar se levantó, coló el café y me despertó de un puntapié. Se había arreglado y yo pensé "es por el santo," pero enseguida me gritó que arriba, que la caminata era larga, pues iríamos a tierras de sus abuelos, donde a él vendría a recogerlo la muerte. Ante tal afirmación no pude evitar una sonrisa y entonces él, ofuscado, comenzó a dar gritos y vueltas por la casa. No tuve otro remedio que vestir mis mugrientos pantalones, calzar mis horadados y sombrero apretado contra el pecho, declararme listo para partir. . . .

The Man Who Tried to Go to Heaven

. . . even as those who are
condemned to wander the
gray patches of the Universe.

BORIS PASTERNAK

It all started when he turned seventy. I'd never have thought a man that old could be such a pain, and I can't get it out of my mind that it's his fault I'm in this situation. Just when I'd started to come into my own, to grow up really, this basket case lands on me out of the sky. That's why despite myself sometimes I hate him, I loathe him, and when I get this way I try to calm down by telling myself he's not to blame, or not entirely, but then I go crazy again and think You paralytic creep, you heartless old cuss, look what you've done to me. You could have just died like anybody else, but you had to get yourself into this wretched state. You were too wrapped up in yourself to give a thought to me, after I followed you across deserts and swamps, forests and hills, to get to this cold, weird land, a thousand times cursed, that makes my hair stand on end, this spellbound land I wander now, cowering and alone, waiting for my chance to get out of here.

It was the day of his birthday. That morning when it was barely light he got up, made some coffee and kicked me awake. He was all dressed up, "for his saint's day," I thought, but then he barked at me to get up, that we had a long road ahead of us, we were going to the land of his ancestors, where death was going to come and take him away. I couldn't keep back a smile at this, and he started shouting and stomping blindly all over the house. I had no choice but to pull on my grubby trousers and my holey shoes and, with my hat clasped to my chest, declare myself ready to go. But the old man said in a scolding tone that this would be a long trip with no return, so I should pack a bundle of vital necessities. We would need food several times before we got there, so he had filled a sack with yams and mameys, bananas and corn, coconuts and chewing tobacco, all of which I was to carry on my shoulders, but ordering me to carry it all wasn't enough, he insisted that I hold the sack this way or that way to avoid bruising the ripe fruit. So I spent the whole trip shifting the load around, because every time I'd find a comfortable position he'd make me change it. Then, to keep my spirits up I guess, he told me not to worry, at the end of our journey my troubles would be over, because there would be food and fruit aplenty growing wild in the land of his ancestors, where everything had been readied for him to await death. He said he was not the first to set out to die in this place, in fact it was an inviolable family tradition. So those of his stock might scatter across the world wherever they wished, but death would come to them only in this land, for they were destined not merely to die, but to actually rise up into the heavens to their just reward. Seeing the look of surprise and dubiousness on my face, he cuffed me with his left hand, callused from his years at the plow, and said, "Step it up—at this rate we'll never get there."

What he said must have been true, because here we found everything needed to wait for death, or even stay alive and forget about dying. I had never seen fields so well kept, bananas so big, oranges so orange. But it was all so remote from the world, so distant from any houses or the sound of a voice, that there weren't even any birds to sing. Everything was engulfed in greenery: the same species of grass grew twice as tall here as anywhere else, the vines were three times vinier than their kind in other parts. According to him, all this was the work of the spirits who looked after the place, but I thought the ground was most likely this fertile thanks to the bodies of all those old people who had come here to die; respectful as I was in words, I had never believed the part about going up to the sky. At most, all the spirits had to do was a little plowing to coax the plants, delirious from all that compost, to grow in furrows.

So we had no need to do anything but eat, sleep and relieve ourselves as we pleased. He told me we needed to wait seven days, and after that he would rise up. I didn't answer, partly so I wouldn't cross him and get cussed out again, and partly because I'd begun to suspect I was dealing with a lunatic. A whole week went by, the best week of my warped existence, because I figured all I'd have to do was bury him when he died and find my way home by going back in the direction we came from.

On the seventh day, sure enough, he awoke with deep circles under his eyes. Death was flitting across his lined face, his hands were trembling uncontrollably. He dug out a candle he had brought with him, lit it, then fell on his knees invoking God and all the saints with passionate prayers in a foreign tongue. He ordered me to stand back so the whirlwind from his take-off wouldn't hurl me against one of the nearby trees. I did as I was told. This was getting boring until I noticed the ground moving beneath his knees. At that moment his face looked as mournful as the head of a fish pulled out of water, except his was covered with red blotches. Suddenly he started to lift off, as a cold, foul wind began to blow. Several trees were ripped from the ground roots and all, and as I watched he rose up, still kneeling, until he was out of sight.

That was when my misfortunes began in earnest. If he had never come back, I might even have felt grateful to him for that week of food and freedom. But he did. I had sat down a few minutes after his departure to eat some breakfast when I heard a rustling in the distance. A bird, I thought absently, but then remembered there weren't any in these parts, so I glanced up to see what it could be. I hadn't long to wonder, because the sound rapidly grew deafening. I stood up, a bite of orange halfway down my throat, and saw him shoot back to earth. He thumped up a huge cloud of dust, and at first I thought he'd been killed by the tremendous impact of the fall, but he began to moan and then called out begging to have water sprinkled on his neck. I didn't do that, in fact I ran off and waited for death to put him out of his misery, but now he was desperately screaming for me to come to his aid, because it turned out only his legs had been shattered. "Give me some help here, you prick!" he called, enraged at his crash.

From then on the plants didn't grow as large, and even the size of their fruit gradually diminished. Finally all that was left, scattered on the ground, were a few squashed oranges and soggy leaves. It seemed as though one night while we were asleep the spirits had returned and undone the furrows, broken up the plots and tamped down the ground, because our surroundings were transformed into a hard, rocky plain. Now I had to stay close by and do everything for him, since he was paralyzed from the fall and never recovered. His legs went soft, and even though I tried to fix him up by tying two long branches onto his legs as splints, every time I hoisted him up by the armpits he'd fall back down and call me a murderer

and a wretch, thinking I was trying to fuck with him. I've had plenty of vengeful impulses, all right, because it would have been best if he had just died a normal death, and I can't help wondering what misdeeds the old man must have committed long ago to be denied entry into heaven. Now when I set out, parched with thirst, on long, futile searches for fruit that's always scarcer, smaller and harder to find, I think up ways to get even with him. I spike his papaya with poisonous seeds, or his coconut milk with toxic sap. Half-dazed now, he doesn't seem to notice, and just swallows whatever I put in his mouth. I used to torment him by twisting his legs like a rag doll's, but when I saw he couldn't feel it, I started putting scorpions down his shirt, because the top half of his body still has sensation and he can feel them sting, and he calls me an ingrate and an abuser, but he can't fight back now.

And yet I haven't deserted him, because despite everything I feel kind of sorry for him, and because a few days ago he let me know he's determined to go up again. He thinks he's atoned for his trespasses, and he says that people who are rejected the first time can try again. Except that while they needed to spend seven days in the enchanted land before the first try, if they're not admitted to paradise they have to wait seven years to try again.

He's become quieter, more decent. He doesn't yell. I can barely tell he's breathing, even though we sleep huddled together to keep the chill off our bones. So I'm still here: it's been five years, and this time, if he lifts off, I know he won't come back. And not until then will I leave this cursed land. I'll do it walking backward and blindfolded to keep from seeing where my footsteps fall. I won't uncover my eyes until I hear birds singing, so that even if I tried, I could never return.

The Singer Machine

René Depestre | Translated by Anita Sagástegui from French (Haiti)

René Depestre often refers to himself as a "banyan-man." Like the tree with multiple, aerial roots that grow back into the ground to become other trees, so has Depestre's nomadic life and work grown multidimensional roots. Poet, essayist, and novelist, his writing is never meek—his words are intense, his images fluctuating between the magical and the surreal, and even in the softest of his poetic verses he manages to leave the reader shivering somewhere between ecstasy and despondent sadness.

Born in Haiti in 1926, Depestre published his first collection of poetry at nineteen. Then an "angry youth," he ardently believed (though a little naively he admits now), that as a poet it was his duty to manifest the beauty and ugliness of life, the real and the surreal, love and revolution into verse for the masses. During this time he passionately aligned himself with the Négritude movement, Communism, and Surrealism, (all of them he would just as passionately reject later), which he explored, along with his own Haitian, Creole, and African heritage through his work.

His most important and influential work began in the seventies when he was living in Cuba, invited there by his great friend, the poet Nicolás Guillén. It was during these years that he experienced a personal revolution, as his hopes for utopia disintegrated with the rise of Stalin as well as what Depestre considered Fidel Castro's betrayal of their credo's original ideals. Disillusionment turned into despair, citing "poetry could no longer breathe" under this deformed communist agenda. He felt responsible, guilty even, for the many verses he had dedicated in support of the movement.

Depestre's collection *Poète á Cuba* not only expresses this dispair, but carries him back to reflections of his youth—the seeds of the magical novels he would be lauded for in the '80s and '90s. Anyone familiar with Depestre's work will recognize the prevalence of the Singer sewing machine. His childhood was not easy. His mother, whom he adored, struggled on her own to feed and educate her five children. It was with her Singer sewing machine that his mother eked out a living for her family, and for them it became a symbol of reverence while paradoxically a monstrous symbol of how dangerously close they came to poverty. Thus, in "The Singer Machine," Depestre brings her ferociously to life, as "she" staves off hunger and guards her territory.

Though Depestre writes in a lilting formal French, he suffuses his writing with Creole. In translating Depestre's work I was aided by his very own definition of what Haitian Creole is: "Often there is a tendency to reduce Haitian Creole to a mere deformation of the French language, or at least, to patois. Rather, [Haitian] Creole is a complex linguistic system in which African syntax and French words astutely weave together." Aware of this, I took an organic approach to translating the poems, listening for Depestre's unforced folding of evocative French words into a nonwestern rhythm. My hope is that I have recreated this union of languages in the English translation.

Original Text: René Depestre, *Poète á Cuba*.
Paris: Pierre-Jean Oswald, 1976.

La Machine Singer

à Mario de Andrade

Une machine Singer dans un foyer nègre
arabe, indien, malais, chinois, annamite,
ou dans n'importe quelle maison sans
boussole du tiers-monde
c'était le dieu lare qui raccommodait
les mauvais jours de notre enfance.
Sous nos toits son aiguille tendait
des pièges fantastiques à la faim,
son aiguille défiait la soif.
La machine Singer domptait des tigres
la machine Singer charmait des serpents
elle bravait paludismes et cyclones
et cousait des feuilles à notre nudité.
La machine Singer n'était pas tombée

des dernières pluies du ciel :
elle avait quelque part un père,
une mère, des tantes, des oncles,
et avant même d'avoir des dents pour mordre
elle savait se frayer un chemin de lionne.
La machine Singer n'était pas toujours
une machine à coudre attelée jour et nuit
à la tendresse d'une fée sous-développée.
Parfois c'était une bête féroce
qui se cabrait avec des griffes
et qui écumait de rage
et inondait la maison de fumée
et la maison restait sans rythme ni mesure
la maison ne tournait plus autour du Soleil
et les meubles prenaient la fuite

The Singer Machine

for Mario de Andrade

A Singer machine in a black family's home
or Arab, Indian, Malay, Chinese, Annamese
any wayward, third-world home
she was the household god that rearranged
the terrible days of our childhood.
Beneath our roofs her needle set
magnificent traps to catch hunger,
her needle defied thirst.
The Singer machine tamed tigers
the Singer machine charmed serpents
she braved cyclones and malaria
she sewed together leaves to clothe our
       naked bodies.
The Singer machine didn't fall

with the last of heaven's rains:
somewhere out there she had a father,
a mother, aunts and uncles,
and even before she had teeth to bite with
she knew how to clear a path fit for a lioness.
The Singer machine wasn't always
a sewing machine harnessed day and night
to the tenderness of a primitive fairy
       godmother.
At times she was a ferocious beast
rearing her claws
foaming with rage
and inundating our home with smoke
leaving the house without rhythm
       or measure

et les tables surtout les tables
qui se sentaient très seules
au milieu du désert de notre faim
retournaient à leur enfance de la forêt
et ces jours-là nous savions que Singer
est un mot tombé d'un dictionnaire de proie
qui nous attendait parfois derrière les portes
une hache à la main !

our home no longer revolved around the sun
and all the furniture ran away
and the tables, especially the tables
who felt so alone
in the middle of our desert of famine
returned to their childhood forest
and in those days we knew that Singer
was a word fallen from a dictionary of prey
that sometimes lurked behind the doors
      an ax in hand!

The Greatest Rabbi on Earth

Denis Baldwin-Beneich　|　Translated by Willard Wood from French (France)

The story begins with a man living beside a pond. He has no idea why he is living there, or who the woman is who is looking after him, or why the two children who trail after her are masquerading as his own. Clearly this is the territory of midlife crisis—and familiar territory to any reader enmeshed in a daily routine, after the choices that brought him or her there have been lost in the haze of time.

What begins in silence, and puzzled wonder, and metaphysical speculation spins wildly out of control as the narrator, Yukel, tries to recover his identity and reassume his fate. He finds himself traveling to Brooklyn in a white stretch limo to challenge Rabbi Schneerson. He is briefly acclaimed as the messiah, but after the ensuing theatrics

and theology, blasphemy and even bloodshed, it is time for Yukel to reassess.

In the excerpt that follows, which is the novel's opening chapter, the narrator is just awakening to his situation. The mist is burning off. The details of his predicament are coming into focus. Very soon the characteristics of his speech become apparent. He likes shtick. If the first paragraph is fairly straight narration, and the second is mock-Biblical in tone, the third proves that we have been set up for a classic vaudeville punch line: "Because you call this living?"

This voice that swerves from register to register is the salient feature of Baldwin-Beneich's writing here, and it is certainly the main concern of the translator. Fortunately, the expression of Jewish culture in English has a long history. If the narrator kvetches with God, or plays the wisenheimer, it doesn't come as unfamiliar to the reader. The comedians who worked the summer resorts in the Catskills have left their mark on our popular culture, and it is entirely appropriate for Yukel to borrow their accents, which he does periodically throughout the selection.

He will also swoop to poetic heights, often with very little transition, as when he describes the fog lifting off the pond, or the sudden flight of a great blue heron. His references draw largely on the Bible. When he thinks of the Shulamite, as he calls her, the woman who cares for him, his all-but wife, he frankly borrows words from the "Song of Solomon," as if no others could do justice to her beauty.

At times borscht-belt comedian and at times the rapt bridegroom of the "Song of Songs," he becomes at other times the logic-chopping Talmudic scholar of Yiddish fiction, spinning out incomprehensible metaphysical arguments, whose only force derives from their fluidity and assurance of delivery.

Yet the translator has to avoid confining Yukel too closely within his Jewishness. There are many entirely secular passages and any number of quiet references to a wider European culture.

In this chapter, the passive narrator is mainly taking stock of his external circumstances, but he is also, through the successive voices he adopts, discovering his inner resources, and it is this which sets in motion the ground-swell of rebellion that will erupt in later chapters as manic and transgressive action. It is not then simply a question of capturing the style of Baldwin-Beneich's prose. By accurately reproducing the register of Yukel's voices, the translator brings the reader to an understanding of the range and versatility of Yukel's character, but also its fragmentation and disjointedness, as he stands at the threshold of a major life crisis.

Original Text: Denis Baldwin-Beneich, *Le plus grand rabbin du monde*. Paris: Denoël, 2002.

Le plus grand rabbin du monde

« Qu'un rabbin sans barbe vaut
mieux qu'une barbe sans rabbin »

DICTON HASSIDIQUE

Depuis quelque temps déjà, je me réveille aux premières lueurs de l'aube. Le jour n'est pas encore là. Sa lumière demeure incertaine, voilée, inconstante et lointaine, visible et invisible tout à la fois. Sans quitter le lit, je regarde par la fenêtre l'obscurité de la nuit se diluer lentement dans les vapeurs qui remontent de l'étang vers le ciel. Après ça, je me lève, sans bruit ou presque mais curieusement tout entouré de ce vacarme intime si propre à la vraie solitude. Je prépare mon café et je sors enfin, pieds nus dans l'herbe froide et lourde de rosée, m'asseoir dans un large et inconfortable fauteuil en bois. Je garde la tasse de café fumant bien serrée entre mes deux mains. Je grelotte. Je ne me couvre pas pour autant. Mon corps transi se réchauffera bientôt, je le sais, comme tous les matins, à la lumière qui s'achemine progressivement vers moi. Je me laisse aller à la contemplation des choses.

Je suis le premier homme à mettre un pied dans ce monde. Et le fauteuil de bois dans lequel je suis installé est un trône placé à la droite de Dieu.

S'Il était là, assis auprès de moi, et moi tout près de Lui, ce serait mieux, bien sûr. Les brumes de ma solitude en seraient irisées. Il me demanderait : « Tu vis là ? » et je Lui répondrais : « Parce que Tu appelles ça vivre, Toi ? »

Mais les nuées s'élèvent d'abord de la terre tandis qu'autour des arbres des pâleurs obscures, nouées comme à des faveurs, se défont et c'est tout.

Les oiseaux dorment encore....

The Greatest Rabbi on Earth

*"That a rabbi without a beard is
better than a beard without a rabbi."*

HASIDIC PROVERB

For some time now I have been waking up at the first streak of dawn. Day hasn't come yet. The light is still uncertain, veiled, inconstant and far-off, visible and invisible all at once. Lying in bed, I watch the nighttime darkness through the window as it is slowly diluted in the vapors rising skyward off the pond. Then I get up, almost without a noise, but oddly enveloped by the intimate roar so characteristic of true solitude. I make myself coffee and step outside, my feet bare in the cold and dew-soaked grass, to sit in a large, uncomfortable wooden armchair. I hold my steaming cup of coffee tightly in my hands. My teeth chatter. But I don't put on more clothes. My chilled body will warm up soon, I know, as it does every morning in the light that gradually makes its way toward me. I let myself go to contemplation.

I am the first man to set foot on this earth. And the wooden armchair on which I sit is a throne placed at the right hand of God.

If He were here, sitting right next to me, and I were sitting right next to Him, that would be best, of course. The mists of my solitude would shine prismatically. He would ask me: "Do you live here?" And I would say: "Because You call this living?"

But the fog rises from the earth toward the sky, while pale shadowy forms, knotted like favors around the trees, loosen and are gone.

The birds are still asleep. I picture them hunched up, bodies in a ball, beaks tucked under their wings, while over their heads, as over mine, reigns an impeccable silence, woven from the wind's irregular breath and the leaves' rustling.

At one end of the sky a few clouds are visible, a very few, almost stationary. It looks as though they're waiting for a signal to start moving. The sun breaks the horizon, and a billowy tide arrives from nowhere, passing silently overhead, heavy and endless. There were three clouds a moment ago, and now I count 20,000 or more, massed together like King David's army.

And from every direction I hear the uninterrupted chittering of birds, those angels of good and evil. No matter how I crane my neck, scanning the tree canopy around the pond, I can never see them. Except once. It was a great blue heron. Noiselessly unfurling in air, it passed into the sky as fluidly as a long silk banner, its presence so majestic as to be incomprehensible. Its outspread wings blotted out the vanishing point of the landscape until the bird itself became the landscape, from which my eyes could no longer turn. I thought at first it was a vision, perhaps because I had not heard the beating of its wings. It seemed the sky was under it, and the bird had passed into my gaze, like a hand coming to rest on your eyelids. Then, after describing a lazy circle over the water, the heron disappeared, leaving me in a state of pure enchantment.

"O Lord, if you were to rend the heavens and descend to earth . . ." I thought, for there is nothing in this world that does not have its correspondent in the extrasensory world, and not even a single blade of grass—or so it is said—that does not have its constellation in the sky.

The Almighty, author of all miracles, had manifestly intended this heron for a sign.

So why did he send me just the one?

But let's forget God and His manifold bounties and get back to my overriding concern, because I desperately need to know His plans for me. I have been here, for instance, in this unknown place for quite some time already, perhaps two or three months. But I don't know exactly because I haven't been counting. And it would be absurd to do so. What would I count? The days and days, more numerous than the fingers of my two hands? And to what purpose? All I know is that there are mornings that I witness with astonishment, and silences that would shake a Trappist monk.

At the same time, I've been doing better recently. It's getting better, much better. Or else I'm getting used to it. But used to what I couldn't say.

My situation, at least what I can grasp of it—because how do you identify with something that escapes you?—seems to share many features of an ordinary, humdrum convalescence, and yet it still causes me considerable worry. I choose to call it "worry" so as not to terrify myself, but then misfortunes are always more threats than they are punishments. I notice things every day around me, ridiculous details, that when added up do not seem normal. I am left perplexed, which in other circumstances might strike me as comic. But mostly I still have no idea what I am doing here, in the middle of these impenetrable woods, facing this pond that shines in the sun like a silver coin dropped in the grass, left to observe the passing hours and their colorful shadows. No idea, none. Literally none.

And anyone else in my position would have no more idea than I do. I'm quite sure of it.

Am I supposed to rest? Does someone intend for me to rest? Rest from what, Lord?

Yet it seems to me that being somewhere, at a minimum, implies being somewhere. My ancestors from Lithuania—now who could have told me this?—lived in miserable conditions. To make a profit at begging, they had to walk more than twenty miles a day before returning to their village. But at least they had a village. And that's something. They complained about it, sure. But what about me, what should I be saying? My situation, when examined closely, is hardly more brilliant. It might even be Euclidean. Let's say that I am at a point. We'll call it a point for want of anything better. Defined as that which has no part. Therefore I am nowhere, neither in these parts nor in any other. This is confirmed to me each day at nightfall when I find the question I had asked myself the day before no closer to solution. And yet if I sit down every morning facing this pond, it is because my entire being is in fact somewhere facing a pond. In consequence, and with respect to the pond, I am nowhere, absolutely. Whether it's this pond or another, all things considered, hardly changes the problem. So I am not just lost, I'm well and truly lost, and isn't there some comfort in that? Well no, I don't think so. And since no one tells me anything and I have no knack for calculating my position on earth by measuring the course of the stars in the sky, there's a good chance I will stay like this a long time beneath the mute and starry vault of heaven, myself mute from ignorance and astonishment.

And was there really any call, even if it was only to increase an already abundant solitude, to saddle me with a full family, wife and children included? Incredible, but true. A boy and a girl, no less. Were I a Jewish grandmother, seeing there was at least one boy in the family, I would cry out: "Honor is served!" Except that I am not a Jewish grandmother and I don't recognize either one of them as mine. I'm talking about the children.

This family, which is brazenly passing itself off as my own—although I never that I can recall expressed a wish to be surrounded by my family—is quite simply a mystery. Another in a string of mysteries. And while there are mysteries of far greater importance, I concede, this one preoccupies me for a good portion of my waking hours, more than is in fact reasonable. It may seem facetious to say or else a bald exaggeration, but the truth is that I have not caught the names of either of the children. And as for their mother, I am left in perplexity: does she or does she not wear a wig? Were she in point of fact my wife, would I not know her better, very much better?

Yet she is as beautiful as Tirzah, comely as Jerusalem, this woman who pretends to be mine.

Terribly strange and strangely beautiful, as though beauty itself walked ahead of her, announcing a being that is simply unimaginable. Each time I see her, I feel a double blow to my heart. Her silhouette reaches me as part human and part angel. An "angel-stranger," I want to say when I first see her arrive at the pond, the fire of her black hair kindled by the light of morning, the shattering nakedness of her whole body behind her veil magnified by the grace of her gentle movements. And there I am, arrested in contemplation of her, a David without a harp. Often she is carrying a holy book under one arm, which she flings in my face without explanation but also without cruelty. The gesture is profane, but the offering is pious. I'm not fooled. She doesn't treat me like the worst of her dogs, but that's all that can be said. I hurriedly open the book and search among the pages left to us by ancient and obscure rabbis from Galicia, Bohemia, or Hungary for the meaning of this lovely and unspeaking face. And when I suddenly discover that this *Treatise on the Soul of Life* is about none other than the angel of love, the one who flies fast, the one who is a thousand times more rapid than the angel of serenity, then I don't know what to think. If she is toying with me, then she has definitely got the upper hand. Subdued, I lay the book down on my knees, raise my eyes toward her, and look at her as though she had just appeared for the first time. And I blush.

The truth is that I'd gladly forgive her the children if in exchange she would consent to be my wife.

"How lovely are thy feet in sandals," I would like to announce whenever we find ourselves together on the shores of the pond, in this enclosed garden, over which she rules like a fountain.

The children, when it comes to that, can always be immolated to Saturn, as the Carthaginians used to do.

"The contours of thy hips are like necklaces, the work of the hands of a cunning workman."

And when the Carthaginians had none, they went out and bought them.

"Thy navel is like a round goblet, which wanteth not spiced wine."

Besides, and to go no farther afield, did not our own Abraham, that exalted father, set just such an example by accepting without hesitation the sacrifice of his son Isaac?

"Thy belly is like an heap of wheat, set about with lilies."

"Thy breasts" well I'm also ready "are like two young roes" to accept the sacrifice. And, "twins of a gazelle" without hemming and hawing either.

I am quite ready.

At times I tell myself that this surprisingly beauti-ful woman, standing right there in front of me, must be none other than the reincarnation of Abishag the Shulamite, that very one who should be warming my icy body with her caresses. But as she does nothing of the sort, not even close, I also tell myself perhaps it is not she. Watching her at other times I feel that she radiates a horrible glow, dreadful and unreal, as though a halo of cold light shimmered around her. Yet it's one and the same person, endowed with the same irrecusable beauty. In any case, I don't remember ever having married such a person. No matter how I ransack my oldest memo-ries, or my most vainglorious dreams, I find no nuptial canopy held above our heads, neither hers, nor mine. No chuppah, nothing. Not the slightest rabbi with perfumed beard singing at our ceremony, no echo of rejoicing, no tribal dances, no glass crushed underfoot to avert the evil eye, nothing, nothing, nothing, only emptiness, the blank moment, and the whistling silence that persists and pervades it.

When I stop and consider, naturally, I have to say the whole story makes no sense, because anyone can forget his wedding, but his wedding night? Unless there was a wedding but no wedding night. Has such a thing ever happened? You would have to suppose that it has. But why should I be its living exemplar?

I glance at my left hand resting on the arm of my chair. I'm not wearing a wedding ring. I look at hers hanging at her side. It looks like the wing of a bird embroidered with mother-of-pearl stitches. Her fingers are bare except for a slender gold ring around the distal phalange of the auricular. It's strange, that thin band around the end of her little finger, and enigmatic, but basically we are equal in this respect. So there was no wedding.

When the fluid gold of morning spreads over her features or a russet shadow crosses her face, momentarily dimming her triumphant beauty, I see a quiet and incom-prehensible gentleness in her, perhaps an expression of her rigorous indifference. Then her eyes grow still, like doves beside a watercourse, and her lips, pale from corner to corner, rediscover the vanished smile of what appears to be a past ecstasy. I may be getting the context wrong.

There are days when I see in her a fleeting resemblance to Saint Theresa, the one by Bernini, at the height of her physical or mystical trance. Hard to say which, as the two ecstasies may commingle during one and the same flight of the soul, by reason of jolts, palpitations, and other pressures of the body, which in this particular case, as I'm well aware, I've contributed little to.

And to crown it all, every time that I'm gripped by some vague reminiscence, or that a chance word or color or odor brings her whole being to the tip of my tongue, her face will suddenly change and post an unmistakable "Go! Get back to Egypt!" that always catches me by surprise and chills my blood. At other times her rebuff is simpler and more secular, a "Come back tomorrow and I'll tell you everything . . ." that seems to hold out a promise, but I've already stopped believing her.

A long while after throwing the holy book in my face, and when the afternoon shadows have lengthened to the point of losing all shape, she does sometimes address me. In accents that owe as much to English as to Yiddish she calls me "Yukel," invariably startling me because of course my name is not Yukel. Then she will ask in a desperately neutral voice whether I feel all right, and before I even have time to answer she will turn away to do something else. Burst out laughing maybe. Though I hope not. Because if each of us goes off to laugh on his own without ever admitting it to the other, or offering to share in his good humor, a practice wherein resides, it seems to me, the charm of married life, then there is definitely something wrong between us.

But she just turns away and that's all. Her back is not shaking.

Oh! If only I dared to grab her by the ankles and pull her toward me!

She is an angel and no doubt of it, "my turtledove, my perfect one." But there are bad angels just as beautiful as she. Every day she looks after me assiduously and with benevolence like an old-fashioned servant, like Abishag the Shulamite in fact, but minus the willing young virgin laying her warm, naked body against my frozen breast. And still I can't shake off the notion that her obstinacy in performing little acts of kindness might serve her just as well to slit my throat, if she were ever to abandon the rigorous indifference that she wears so becomingly.

As to the children, the least you can say is that they possess nothing of their mother's perfect grace. And it makes a certain sense. Given that she is not my wife, why should she be the mother of my children? They exhibit, the children, a sporadic affection toward me that I am at loss to respond to. Should I open my arms wide? Or should I keep them at a distance? What am I to do? I don't want to seem unnecessarily cruel, but at the same time I don't want to love them back just because they've sniffed and groaned all day to make me think they are sick. Both of them, the boy and the girl, look like chickens, with that bird's long, thin neck, and the wounded gait of those who are going nowhere in particular. They wear the same thing, little boxy shirts and overlong shorts so dull in color that they could be gray. And their skin is pale, their joints almost blue. I really can't find in them any resemblance to me. When the two of them start coughing at the same time, coughing so as to tear their lungs

out, their tongues stiff, their eyes round and bulging, the exercise going on so long that the birds fly up to their branches and are quiet, she will at length intervene in the voice of an inspired priestess, marking each syllable distinctly: "Se-ren-i-ty! Se-ren-i-ty!" It has the immediate effect of paralyzing them. Me, it takes by surprise too. And afterwards they calm down, they wander off to spit their phlegm elsewhere. If they cried, their crying would bring us closer, somewhat. It would inevitably affect me, because tears have merit, and I know of no one who is genuinely unmoved by them. Besides, did not Rabbi Isaac of blessed memory teach us that Israel's deliverance hangs on tears alone? But the eyes of these two children, may God forgive me, are as dry as seashells.

At the first sign of evening, the birch trees and the beeches around the pond take on the vermilion tint of the setting sun. The towering pines raise themselves up to catch the highest light in the sky, while their branches gather the first shadows of night. Then a bird sends out his call, speaking his song precisely: "Weep, poor Will. Weep, poor Will." His diction is so clear that there is no mistaking the sense of his couplet. But then, my name is not William either. The Shulamite, rather than savor with me the wonder of this distinct voice, which travels through the darkening woods for our ears alone, reads this as the signal to leave. She gathers her little band together, orders her children to go to the car, then signals me to do the same.

And every night, I agree to it without a fuss. After all, you never know.

The children ride in front. They are so thin they don't even have to push to make room for themselves. Two matchsticks in a box. The back seat is for me alone. I don't brag about it. The Shulamite drives fast but I'm not afraid. It's a short trip on a back road. First we go through a field, raising impressive clouds of dust that, whipped by the wind, catch up with the car and pass ahead of us. Then we wind along the Gentiles' narrow asphalt road for half a mile or so. The roadway is gouged along its whole

length by the winter's frost. On the left are trees, and on the right are trees, with a vague yellowish expanse at one point that looks like an abandoned meadow, bordered by a long, gap-toothed fence, and filled with tall grasses that wave to the horizon in the slanting evening light. The few electric poles along the road are hardly noticeable, their black wires hung from crest to crest already blending with the night. The Shulamite veers abruptly off the road onto a dirt track. We arrive in another cloud of dust.

And here is the red house, hidden in a dip at some distance from the turn-off. You would never notice it driving by but practically have to stop right in front of it to see it. That's where they live, or hide, when they aren't with me, and where they drive me every night for dinner. With its four small windows in the front, the house is modest in appearance but widens out toward the back, suggesting the discreet and well-appointed structures of an earlier age. It is painted a very particular shade of red that I have never seen anywhere else except in the Swedish countryside, a red that brims with light yet only truly vibrates when it is painted on wood and set off by a very blue sky. And the sky is still very blue when the dinner bell sounds for me.

The ceremonial is brief.

I sit alone at table, just as I do in the back of the car. The Shulamite serves me my dinner. Once she has set the plate in front of me, she withdraws and stands a few steps away. To see that I eat my herring, maybe? On some days there aren't even bagels. The children stand a bit further away, like little waiters in training. I suppose it must annoy her to watch me push the rings of sliced onion methodically to the edge of my plate. She must think that, unlike the Hebrews in the desert, I don't miss the onions they ate during their captivity in Egypt. In any case, she is mistaken. The onions would in no wise soften my captivity. And then again she may not care at all, either about the onions or my captivity. When she fills my wine glass, I again notice the slender ring around the distal phalange of her auricular, and though I try to pay no attention it affects me.

I empty my glass in one gulp hoping she will refill it. But once I have put the last piece of herring in my mouth she comes and stands behind my chair, grabbing it by the back to let me know it's time to get up. So I get up from the table. What am I supposed to do? I understood a long time ago that I was never going to get dessert in that house.

The three of them accompany me in the car back to the pond. The return trip is no gayer than the trip out. Then they put me to bed, and each in turn gives me a kiss, she on my hand and the other two on the hem of my shirt. She shuts off the light but stays a few short moments in the darkened room, busy with something or other. If only she would walk back toward my bed for a fugitive caress, a quick, meaning squeeze, a kiss in the dark, with or without the tongue, anything to the purpose. But no. I think she's praying, the killjoy, or else casting a spell on me to make this night worse than all the others.

Eventually she closes the door and the three of them go away.

Their steps moving off across the grass are inaudible, but I soon hear the sound of car doors opening in the fresh night and being slammed shut one after the other, often four or five times in a row, I suppose because the children can't manage to close their doors properly the first time.

I sleep alone in the gray and white cabin facing the pond. The first time I saw the place, I was moved to say "*A chico pajarillo, chico nidillo,*" for a small bird, a small nest. I was in a good mood and still disposed to make jokes. Of course I had no idea that the little nest would close in on me. How can you even imagine a nest closing in on you? I'd noticed that the cabin had only one bed, one chair, and one table big enough to put two elbows on. I must have said "Charming!" two or three times and then not known what else to say.

At night there is only me and from time to time the song of the weep-poor-Will. I say that I'm alone at night but I am probably exaggerating. It may be true, it may be false. Anyway, who can be absolutely sure of being entirely alone at night? Isn't the whole world full of nasty, harmful spirits?

They may be invisible, but you can force them to appear if you know how. What I do, for instance, is to spread a layer of sifted ashes around my bed at night, and in the morning I find the whole area marked with what look like chicken tracks. If I were absolutely determined to see these spirits, it would obviously be more complicated. Following the prescription of the blessed Talmud, I'd take the firstborn of the firstborn of the litter of a black cat, roast it in the fire, reduce it to a powder, and place the powder in my eyes. Then I would truly see them.

At other points during the night, I feel jostling presences beyond my closed eyelids. I recognize Queen Lilith of the Demons among them, accompanied by members of her court. They are trying to get me excited. They know that I am cruelly deprived of a female partner. Of course they make the best of it. They provoke me by all sorts of tickling to perform the sexual act in aerial contortions that even I am surprised at, with the sole purpose of collecting the sperm that thus falls into the void, and even lower than the void. Which is exactly how demons reproduce. So you shouldn't be surprised to find them in quantity at people's houses, just as they are found at mine.

Am I being watched?
      To prevent me from running away?
      And where would I run away to?
      And leave her behind?

"I'm so happy to be here, to take in this dusting of ideas."

François Ayroles | Translated by Edward Gauvin from French (France)

The first comic I ever saw by François Ayroles was his six-panel distillation of Proust in the first Oubapo anthology (Oubapo is to comics what Oulipo is to literature). With his flair for formal invention, Ayroles compresses the search for lost time to a silent, characterless view of Marcel's apartment. Through a small window in the top left corner, a glimpse of a house is slowly veiled by a growing tree gone bare by the final panel when, in a clever *mise-en-abyme,* a canvas on an easel both reproduces the initial panel and obscures our view of the now-empty room. Objects come and go, each one—gloves, puppets, champagne flutes—freighted with semiotic significance. With this single page, Ayroles rescues the cheapened image and restores the picture-word exchange rate to its proverbial 1:1000. Here, I thought, was an artist to watch.

Born in 1969, Ayroles attended the *École supérieure de l'image* in Angoulême, home to the world's largest comics festival every January. He has worked with several major comics companies—including Casterman, and Denoël, who published what remains his only book available in the U.S., an adaptation with Ted Benoît of Raymond Chandler's *Playback* (Arcade, 2006)—but the bulk of his output remains with L'Association, best known here for Marjane Satrapi's *Persepolis*. The success story of L'Association is unique, as both its founding members and many of its authors have proved premier talents in contemporary French comics.

Among Ayroles's graphic novels are *Incertain Silence*, a paean to Buster Keaton, and *Le Jeu de dames*, an initiation story with surreal touches. His most recent novel, *Les Amis*, an official selection at Angoulême 2009, expands on a short story in his first collection *Travail rapide et soigné* (Quick'n'Classy Clips), from which the following piece is also taken. It's in these shorter works, I think, that Ayroles's ingenuity sparkles; his irony is evident in wit and experiment, matched by meticulous linework. "I'm So Happy..." is kind of a highbrow hit-and-run skit that comedy has largely abandoned to comics. The couple by the title conjures *The World As Will and Representation* ("Short men have a decided inclination for tall women, and *vice versa*"), and in the penultimate panel of the first page, is Arthur admiring the elephant's intellect? With sly exuberance, Ayroles launches several clay pigeons at once—women's magazines, serial killers—and takes satirical aim. How about that pelican?

Original Text: François Ayroles, "Je suis heureuse d'être là, de recevoir toute cette poussière d'idées," from *Travail rapide et soigné*. Paris: L'Association, 2007.

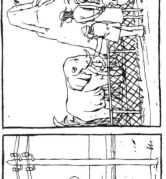

"WE ALL RECALL THE STRING OF MURDERED LITTLE GIRLS THAT EARNED ISABELLE FIELDFLOWER THE NICKNAME "ZAZA, THE DAY-CARE STRANGLER," AS WELL AS INTERNMENT IN AN INSANE ASYLUM."

"I'M SO HAPPY TO BE HERE, TO TAKE IN THIS DUSTING OF IDEAS."

A FREE WOMAN NOW, ZAZA FILLS US IN ON LIFE WITH HER NEW HUSBAND, ARTHUR SCHOPENHAUER.

I met Arthur at the clinic. He was being treated for psychosis in the famous homesick wing.

Our honeymoon gave us a chance to deepen our relationship on visits to well-adjusted cultures.

We got along right off the bat, but had to wait until we left the clinic to get married.

"ARTHUR HAS THIS REALLY AMAZING INNER LIFE."

He can spend hours thinking and studying.

"ON HIS END, HE TRIED TO INTRODUCE ME TO HIS SPIRITUAL PREOCCUPATIONS."

"DESPITE HIS EXTREME INTROVERSION, ARTHUR CAME TO SHARE MY APPETITE FOR LIFE."

FOCUS ON PALESTINIAN POETRY

Focus on Palestinian Poetry

EDITOR'S NOTE

The idea of assembling for TWO LINES a group of Palestinian poets, whose work shows at once some of the tendencies of contemporary poetry in Arabic, and the Palestinian specificity coming from a shared history and a shared struggle, occurred to me in the spring of 2008. At the time, I envisioned including poets of the generations and literary constellations beginning with Ghassan Zaqtan (b.1954 in Beit Jala), author of a dozen collections, who has himself edited an important anthology of younger Palestinian poets. The work of Mahmoud Darwish seemed to stand alone, that of a "world" poet at once essentially of his own time, language, nationality and history, and existing in a place (inhabited by poets and readers of many tongues and traditions) apart from it.

Darwish died in August 2008, too young: it then seemed imperative to open this section with a poem of his. In fact, the duovocal "Rita's Winter," in which Darwish revisits personae and situations created in earlier work—the Palestinian Arab poet as lover of a Jewish Israeli woman who is also a soldier, their imagined dialogue—sets out one of the paradigms of contemporary Palestinian poetry: a history larger than that of any individual expressed through narratives of the quotidian and the deceptively personal. This stands alongside, and arises in part from the inescapable fact of exile (and the presence of a not at all imaginary occupying Other) as one of the principal components of contemporary Palestinian writing, a paradoxical but undeniable source of its inspiration. But this energy is not insular; it's also an integral part of the ongoing renaissance of poetry in Arabic (the creation of an Arabic modernism) that began in the circle around the journal *Ch'ir* (Poetry) founded in Lebanon in the 1960s by a circle of poets including the Syrian Adonis (also represented in this volume), a movement that, as the Moroccan poet-critic Abellatif La'abi claims, enlarged poets' angle of vision while revising and recasting their poetic "arsenal." The tropes and cadences of classical Arabic poetry were met, confronted by European ideas of ruptured and new forms, while "new" ways of thinking about aesthetics were reconnected with classical, spiritual, and philosophical sources. Darwish's evolution as a poet permitted Palestinian writers of succeeding generations (how short these generations are!) to go beyond a mythology of exile, of recreating a formerly promised land frozen in idealism and despair, to the expression of an internalized exile which corresponds, as well, to the human condition, an imagination of *al-wattan* (the word "homeland" has been corrupted in American English) as also something internal, intimate, the apotheosis of daily life.

The poets here presented, then, range from Darwish, who would still be in his mid-sixties, and who was part of that renaissance at its inception, to Zaqtan and Ibrahim Nasrallah, born in the mid-1950s, to many poets born in the 1970s, sometimes first published in the Palestinian literary journal *al-Karmel*, founded by Darwish, with first and second books already published in Palestine or elsewhere in the Arab world. They live in Ramallah, in Jerusalem, in Lebanon; they are also journalists, teachers, engineers, activists. Their translators, themselves from Palestine, Iraq, Lebanon, also represent the Arab diaspora—and the enrichment it is now bestowing on American English.

MARILYN HACKER

With the passing of time a feeling of disinterest in discussing the "craft" of translation overtakes me. Translating poetry may not be equal to authoring a new poem but is largely the writing of a poem anew. However, translation remains an aesthetic choice, a reflection of the translator's metaphorical state of mind as it treks deep into song and word, toward the confluence where the dissimilar is one.

I can say that Mahmoud Darwish's "Rita's Winter" is a poem my wife, Hana, guided me towards years ago, and that I occasionally would greet her with: "Good morning Rita." I can add that Rita is a pseudonym for Darwish's Jewish Israeli lover when he was in his twenties and that he had written five or six poems to her throughout the 1960s and '70s before writing this one, his final one for her, in 1992. Rita was made an icon of contemporary Arabic culture through the Lebanese composer and musician, Marcel Khalife, who sang Darwish's poem "Rita and the Rifle" (where love is broken because of the Israeli military service). I can say that Rita signifies an essence of Darwish's poetry, its humanizing of the other, a daring from which Darwish never shied. I can say "Rita's Winter" is a brilliant poem because it exhibits, among many other things, Darwish's use of dialogue, an art he developed until he turned his later poems into plays, without calling them plays.

Ayman Ghbarieh and Nasser Rabah represent the

new Palestinian poetry in its bend toward the individual, quotidian concern away from the highly lyrical diction of Darwish. And while Darwish's presence (through "absence" or "pigeons" for example) can be easily felt, the necessary break from Darwish's giant shadow has already taken hold in Palestinian poetry.

Ghassan Zaqtan (b. 1954), however, is a different matter. To call him a bridge between the younger generation and Darwish's timeless mastery would be an oversimplification. Zaqtan is an avant-garde who was among the first poets to experiment with merging prosody and free verse. He was championed across the Arab world by younger poets who were relieved to delve into the possibilities of new diction that would address daily concerns more intimately, and with a post-Freudian specificity, as I like to call it.

While it is difficult to display Zaqtan's brilliance in just the two pieces included here, between the personal elegy and the collective one, his delicate use of the legend and folktale clearly weaves a private language with mystifying lyrical syntax. He was a close friend of Darwish, who had publicly "bet his money" on Zaqtan's importance to Arabic poetry years ago, a fraternal embrace from one great poet to another.

FADY JOUDAH

شتاء ريتا

ريتا تُرتِّبُ ليْلَ غرفتنا: قليلُ
هذا النبيذُ,
وهذه الأزهارُ أكبرُ من سَريري
فافتحْ لها الشباكَ كي يتعطرَ الليلُ الجميلُ
ضعْ, ههنا, قمراً على الكرسيِّ. ضعْ
فوقَ, البحيرةَ حولَ منديلي ليرتفع النخيلُ
أعلى وأعلى,
هل لبستَ سوايَ؟ هل سكنتْكَ إمرأةٌ
لتُجهشَ كلما التفتْ على جذعي فُروعُكَ؟
حُكَّ لي قدمي, وحُكَّ دمي لنَعْرفَ ما
تُخَلِّفُهُ العواصفُ والسيولُ
مني ومنك...

تنامُ ريتا في حديقة جسمِها
توتُ السياج على أظافرها يُضيءُ المِلحَ في

Rita's Winter

Mahmoud Darwish | Translated by Fady Joudah

Rita arranges our room's night and says: This wine
is little
and these flowers are larger than my bed
open the window for them to perfume the beautiful night
and place, right here, a moon on the chair, and place
there, on top, the lake around my handkerchief, let the palm trees rise
higher and higher . . .
or have you worn other than me? Has another woman dwelled in you
that you sob each time your branches wrap around my trunk?
Scratch my feet, scratch my blood for us to know what
storms and floods leave behind
of you and me . . .

Rita sleeps in her body's garden
the berries on the fence of her nails light up the salt

جسدي. أُحِبُّكِ. نام عصفوران تحت يديَّ...
نامت موجةُ القمح النبيل على تنفُّسها البطيء,
ووردةٌ حمراءُ نامت في الممرِّ,
ونام ليلٌ لا يطولُ
والبحرُ نام أمام نافذتي على إيقاع ريتا
يعلو ويهبط في أشعّة صدرها العاري, فنامي
بيني وبينكِ, لا تغطّي عتمة الذهبِ العميقة بيننا
نامي يداً حول الصدى,
ويداً تُبَعْثِرُ عُزلة الغابات, نامي
بين القميص الفستقيِّ ومقعد الليمون, نامي
فرَساً على رايات ليلة عُرسها...
هَدَأً الصهيلُ
هدأت خلايا النخل في دمنا, فهل كانت هنا
ريتا, وهل كنا معاً؟

... ريتا سترحلُ بعد ساعات وتتركُ ظلَّها
زنزانةً بيضاءَ. أين سنلتقي؟
سألتْ يديها, فالتفتُ إلى البعيد

البحرُ خلف الباب, والصحراءُ خلف البحر, قبِّلني على
شفتيَّ — قالت. قلتُ: يا ريتا, أُرحل من جديد

in my blood. I love you. Two birds slept beneath my hands . . .
The noble wheat wave slept on her slow breathing
a red rose slept in the hallway
a night that isn't long slept
and the sea in front of my window slept to Rita's cadence
rising and falling in the rays of her naked chest
so sleep, Rita, in the middle of me and you and don't cover
the deep golden darkness between us
sleep with one hand around echo and the other
scattering the solitude of the forests
sleep between the pistachio shirt and the lemon seat
like a mare upon the banners of her wedding night . . .
The neighing has quieted
the beehives in our blood have quieted, but was Rita
here, and were we together?

   . . . Rita will depart in a few hours and leave her shadow
as a white prison cell. Where will we meet?
Her hands asked, but I turned toward the distant.
The sea is behind the door, the desert behind the sea, kiss me
on my lips—she said. I said: Rita, why should I depart anew

ما دام لي عِنَبٌ وذاكرةٌ, وتتركني الفصولُ

بين الإشارة والعبارة هاجساً؟
ماذا تقول؟

لا شيءَ يا ريتا, أقلّد فارساً في أغنية
عن لعنة الحب المحاصَر بالمرايا...

عَنّي؟
وعن حُلُمين فوق وسادةٍ يتقاطعان ويهرُبان, فواحدٌ
يستلُّ سكيناً, وآخَرُ يُودِعُ النايَ الوصايا
لا أُدركُ المعنى, تقولُ
ولا أنا, لغتي شظايا
كغياب إمرأةٍ عن المعنى, وتنتحر الخيولُ
في آخر الميدان...

ريتا تحتسي شايَ الصباح
وتقشّر التفاحة الأولى بعشر زنابقٍ,
وتقولُ لي:
لا تقرأ الآن الجريدة, فالطبول هي الطبولُ
والحرب ليست مهنتي. وأنا أنا. هل أنتَ أنتَ؟

as long as I have grapes and memory, and the seasons still leave me
anxious between gesture and phrase?
—What are you saying?
—Nothing, I mimic a horseman in a song
about the curse of a love besieged by mirrors . . .
—About me?
—And about two dreams on the pillow, they intersect and escape so one
draws out a dagger and another bids farewell to what the flute decrees
—I don't get the meaning
—Nor do I, my language is shrapnel
like a woman's absence from meaning, and the horses are in suicide
at the end of the field . . .

      Rita sips the morning tea
and peels the first apple with ten irises
and says: Don't read the newspaper now, the drums are the drums
and war isn't my profession. And I am I. Are you, you?
I am he, I say
who saw a gazelle throw her glitter upon him
and saw his desires stream after you
and saw the two of us bewildered in unison on the bed

أنا هو,
هو من رَآكِ غزالة ترمي لآلِئَها عليه
هو من رأى شهواتِهِ تجري وراءكِ كالغدير
هو من رآنا تائِهَيْن تَوَحَّدا فوق السرير
وتباعدا كتحية الغرباء في الميناء, يأخذُنا الرحيلُ
في ريحِهِ ورقاً ويرمينا أمام فنادق الغرباء
مثل رسائلٍ قُرِئتْ على عجلٍ,
أتأخذني معك؟
فأكونَ خاتم قلبكَ الحافي, أتأخذني معك
فأكون ثوابكَ في بلاد أنجبتْكَ... لِتَصرَعكْ
وأكونَ تابوتاً من النعناع, يحملُ مصرعكْ
وتكونَ لي حيّاً مَيْتاً,

ضاع يا ريتا الدليلُ
والحبُّ مثلُ الموت وَعْدٌ لا يُرَدُّ... ولا يزولُ

... ريتا تُعِدُّ ليَ النهارْ
حجلاً تَجَمَّعَ حول كعب حذائها العالي:
صباح الخير يا ريتا,
وغيماً أزرقاً للياسمينةِ تحت إبطيْها:
صباح الخير يا ريتا,

before we became distant like a greeting between strangers at harbor
then departure carried us like a paper in its wind
and threw us at the doorsteps of hotels like letters read in a hurry.
She says: Will you take me with you: I would
become the ring of your barefoot heart
if you take me with you
I would become your garb in a country that birthed you . . . to perish you
I would become a coffin of mint that carries your doom
and you would become mine, dead and alive . . . ?
O Rita, the guide is lost
and love, like death, is a promise that can't be refused . . . and doesn't vanish

      . . . Rita prepares the morning for me
like two partridges that have gathered around her high-heels:
Good morning Rita
like blue clouds for the jasmine under her armpits
Good morning Rita
like fruit for the light of dawn: O Rita, good morning, Rita
bring me back to my body for the pine
needles to quiet briefly in the blood I abandoned after you. Whenever
I embrace the ivory tower two doves flee my hands . . .

وفاكهة لضوء الفجر: يا ريتا صباح الخير, يا
ريتا أعيديني إلى جسدي لتهدأ لحظةً
إبرُ الصنوبر في دمي المهجور بعدكِ. كلما
عانقتُ برج العاج فرّتْ من يديَّ يمامتان..
قالت: سأرجع عندما تتبدل الأيامُ والأحلامُ... طويلٌ
هذا الشتاءُ, ونحن نحن, فلا تقولي ما أقولُ أنا هي,
هي مَن رأتْكَ معلّقاً فوق السياج, فأنزلتْكَ وضمّدتْكَ
وبدمعها غسلتْكَ, وانتشرتْ بسوسنها عليكْ
ومررتَ بين سيوف إخوتها ولعنة أمها. وأنا هي
هل أنتَ أنتْ؟

... تقوم ريتا
عن ركبتيَّ, تزور زينتَها, وتربطُ شَعرَها بفراشةٍ
فضيةٍ. ذيلُ الحصان يداعب النمشَ المبعثَرْ
كرذاذ ضوء داكن فوق الرخام الأنثويِّ. تعيد ريتا
زرَّ القميص إلى القميص الخردليِّ... أأنتَ لي؟
لكِ, لو تركتِ الباب مفتوحاً على ماضيَّ, لي
ماضٍ أراه الآن يُولد من غيابكِ,
من صرير الوقت في مفتاح هذا الباب, لي
ماضٍ أراه الآن يجلس قُربنا كالطاولة,
لي رغوةُ الصابون,

She said: I will return when the days and the dreams change. But Rita . . . this
winter is long, and we are who we are, so don't say what I tell myself: I am she
who saw me hanging on the fence, brought me down, bandaged
and washed me with her tears, and spread her lily over me
until I passed among her brothers' swords and her mother's curse. I am she
so are you, you?

      . . . Rita gets up
from my knees, visits her beauty, and binds her hair with a silver
butterfly. The horsetail dallies with the freckles that are scattered
like the drizzle of a dark light over the feminine marble. Rita returns
the shirt button to the vinegary shirt . . . and says: Are you mine?
I am yours, I say, if you leave the door open to my past, mine
is a past I see born out of your absence
out of the squeaking time in this door's key, mine
is a past I now see sitting near us like a table
the soap lather is mine
      the salted honey
          the dew
             and the ginger
Rita says: And yours are the stags, if you want, the stags and the plains

والعسلُ المملَّحُ,

والندى,

والزنجبيلُ

ولك الأيائلُ, إنْ أردتَ, لك الأيائلُ والسهولُ

ولك الأغاني, إنْ أردتَ, لك الأغاني والذهولُ

إني وُلدتُ لكي أُحبكْ

فرساً تُرقِّصُ غابةً, وتشُقُّ في المرجان غيبَكْ

ووُلدتُ سيدةً لسيِّدها, فخذْني كي أُصبّكْ

خمراً نهائياً لأشفى منكَ فيكَ, وهاتِ قلبكْ

إني وُلدتُ لكي أُحبكْ

وتركتُ أمي في المزامير القديمة تلعن الدنيا وشعبكْ

ووجدتُ حرّاس المدينة يُطعِمون النارَ حُبّكْ

وأنا وُلدتُ, لكي أُحبكْ

... ريتا تكسِّر جوز أيامي, فتتسع الحقولُ

لي هذه الأرضُ الصغيرةُ غرفةٌ في شارع

في الطابق الأرضيِّ من مبنىً على جبلِ

يُطِلُّ على هواء البحر. لي قمرٌ نبيذيٌّ, ولي حجرٌ صقيلُ

لي حصةٌ من مشهد الموج المُسافِر في الغيوم, وحصةٌ

من سِفْرِ تكوين البداية, حصةٌ من سفر أيّوبٍ, ومن

عيد الحصاد, وحصة مما ملكتُ, وحصة من خبز أمي

and yours are the songs, if you want, the songs and the astonishment
I was born to love you
a mare who makes a forest dance, and carves your unknown in corals
I was born a woman to her man, take me and I will pour you in the glass
of my final wine, and cure myself of you, in you, so come and bring your heart
I was born to love you
I left my mother in the ancient psalms cursing your people and the world
I found the city guards feeding your love to the fire
and I was born, to love you

      . . . Rita cracks the walnut of my days, and the fields expand
and this small earth becomes mine, like a room on the ground floor
in a building on a street on a mountain
that overlooks the sea air. I have a moon of wine, I have a burnished stone
and I have a share in the scene of the waves that travel in clouds, a share
in the scripture of creation, a share in Job's book, and in
the harvest feast, a share in what I owned, and in my mother's bread
a share in the lily of the valley in the poems of ancient lovers
and a share in the wisdom of love: the murdered adores his murderer's face . . .
—O Rita, if only you would cross the river?
—And where is the river?

لي حصة من سوسن الوديان في أشعار عُشّاق قدامى
لي حصة من حكمة العشاق: يَعشَقُ وجهَ قاتله القتيلُ,

لو تعبرين النهرَ, يا ريتا.
وأين النهرُ؟ قالت ...
قلتُ: فيكِ وفيَّ نهرّ واحدٌ,
وأنا أسيلُ دماً, وذاكرةً أسيلُ
لم يترك الحُرّاسُ لي باباً لأدخل, فاتّكأتُ على الأفقْ
ونظرتُ تحتَ,

نظرتُ فوقَ,
نظرتُ حولَ,
فلم أجد
أفقاً لأنظر, لم أجد في الضوء إلا نظرتي
ترتَدُّ نحوي. قلتُ: عُودي مرةً أخرى إليَّ, فقَدَ أرى
أحداً يحاول أن يرى أفقاً يرمّمه رسولُ
برسالةٍ من لفظتين صغيرتين: أنا, وأنتِ
فرَحٌ صغير في سرير ضَيِّقٍ... فرح ضئيلُ
لم يقتلونا, بَعْدُ, يا ريتا, ويا ريتا.. ثقيلُ
هذا الشتاءُ وباردٌ

—In you and me there is one river
and I flow as blood and memory
but the guards left no door through which I can enter
so I leaned on the horizon
and looked below
      above
              around
                       yet couldn't see
a horizon, I found only my gaze in the light
bouncing back to me. I told it: Go back once more, I might see
someone looking for a horizon a prophet renovates
with a message of two small sounds: I and you
are a little joy in a narrow bed . . . a small joy
they haven't killed yet, O Rita . . . Rita, this winter
is heavy, and cold

      . . . Rita sings alone
to the mail of her distant northerly estrangement: I left my mother alone
near the lake, alone, crying over my distant childhood
where each evening she sleeps on the little braid of mine that she has kept.
But I broke my childhood, mother, and came out a woman nourishing her breast

... ريتا تغني وحدَها

لبريد غربتها الشمالي البعيد: تركتُ أمي وحدها

قُربَ البحيرة وحدها, تبكي طفولتيَ البعيدة بعدها

في كل أمسية تنام على ضفيرتيَ الصغيرة عندها

أمي, كسرتُ طفولتي وخرجتُ إمرأةً تربّي نهدها

بفم الحبيب. تدور ريتا حول ريتا وحدها:

لا أرضَ للجسدين في جسد ولا منفىً لمنفىَ

في هذه الغرف الصغيرة, والخروج هو الدخولُ

عبثًا تغنّي بين هاويتين, فلنرحلْ... ليتّضح السبيلُ

لا أستطيع, ولا أنا, كانت تقول ولا تقولُ

وتهدّئُ الأفراسَ في دمها: أمِن أرضٍ بعيدةٌ

تأتي السنونو, يا غريبُ ويا حبيبُ, إلى حديقتكَ الوحيدة؟

خذْني إلى أرض بعيدة

خذْني إلى الأرض البعيدة, أجهشتْ ريتا: طويلُ

هذا الشتاءُ,

وكسرتْ خزف النهار على حديد النافذة

وضعتْ مسدسَها الصغيرة على مسودة القصيدةُ

ورمتْ جوارَبها على الكرسيِّ, فانكسرَ الهديلُ

with the lover's mouth . . .
Rita circles around Rita alone and says:
There is no land for two bodies in one, no exile for exile
in these small rooms, and exit is entry:
We sing between two chasms in vain . . . we should depart and clarify the path
yet I can't and you can't . . . she used to say and not say
while calming the mares in her blood: Is it from a faraway land
that the swallows come, O stranger and lover, to your lonely garden?
Take me to a faraway land
take me to the faraway land, Rita sobbed, this winter
is long . . .
   And she broke the ceramic of the day against the iron windowpane
she placed her handgun on the poem's draft
threw her stockings on the chair, and the cooing broke
and she went barefoot to the unknown, and departure reached me

كمن ينتظرني

حين أذكرُهُ
واقفاً تحتَ ضوءٍ خفيفٍ
كمن ينتظرني لأذكرَهُ
حين أشباحُنا
تهبطُ الليلَ من سلّمٍ في صلاةِ العشاء
على مهل
.........ها..

التراويحُ في إثرها
والتسابيحُ
والنومُ في جنّةِ الراجعين.

.. كمن ينتظرني ليخبرَني:
نحن في خيمة الأربعين.. معاً!

أو لأخبرهُ:
يا أبي
لا دعاةَ لنا في النواحي
لا رواةَ لنا في الكتابِ
ولا تابعين!

Like One Who Waits for Me

Ghassan Zaqtan | Translated by Fady Joudah

When I remember him standing
under a soft light
like one who waits for me to remember him,
when our ghosts
slowly descend from the ladder
of the night slow-
ly descend,
after the evening prayers, the rosary
and the late night prayers
and the sleep in the paradise

of those who return . . .
like one who waits for me to tell me:
We are in the tent together
the one pitched for the fortieth day
of the dead . . . together!
Or maybe so I can tell him:
O father
no one prays for us in these corners
we have no narrators in the books
and no followers!

فكَّر طويلاً في العودةِ إلى هناكْ

فكَّر في العودةِ إلى هناكْ
حيث تركها مصغة
بقميصٍ أزرقَ وكمَّيْن قصيرين

كان هناك رجلٌ يقطعُ الشارعَ, دون أن يلتفت,
بينما خياناتُه تتعثرُ خلفهُ مثلَ كومةٍ من النساء البدينات
فيما "هو" يهبطُ الدّرجاتِ الثلاثَ مُحاذراً أن يصطدمَ
بآنيةِ الزهور المدلَّلة

فكَّر طويلاً في العودةِ
حيث تركها مصغية
بعينين عسليَّتين وقلبٍ مفطور

He Thought Long of Going Back There

Ghassan Zaqtan | Translated by Fady Joudah

He thought of going back there
where he had left her listening
in a blue shirt and short sleeves

There was a man crossing the street without looking
whereas his infidelities were behind him stumbling like a heap
of obese women, whereas he was going down the three steps
careful not to bump into the pampered flower pot

He thought long of going back
where he had left her listening
with honey eyes and a cloven heart

ثمّة أولادٌ يتمرجحونَ بقسوةٍ
على شجيرةِ الخوخ التي لا يتذكرها
بينما "هو" يحاولُ, دون جدوى تقريباً, تبيُّنَ الدرجاتِ
وإبعادَ نباتِ المجنونةِ عن العتبة

عندما, فجأةٌ, قرعَ الجرسُ
الجرسُ القديمُ في العليّةِ,
العليّةِ التي غطّتها أزهارُ المجنونةِ منذُ تلكَ الليلة,
الليلةِ التي قتل فيها الإخوةُ الأحد عشرَ
شقيقتَهُم الوحيدةَ!

A few boys were swinging intensely
from the peach tree he has no memory of
while he was trying, in vain, to discern the steps
and move the bougainvillea pot out of the way

When, suddenly, the bell rang
the ancient bell on the hill
the hill which, since that night, the bougainvillea has covered,
that night when the eleven brothers killed
their only sister.

لماذا علينا أن نعلم عدُوَنا تربية الحمام؟

لماذا علينا أن ندرب عدُوَنا على حركةٍ يدنا في نثر الفتات؟
لماذا علينا أن نصر على أن نُريه كيف يبتسمُ خبزُنا للمناقير ؟
لماذا علينا أن نعلم عدُوَنا تربية الحمام ؟
ربما
لأن الخبزَ إسمُ الله على الأرض
وفي ذاكرةِ الحمام طوفانٌ قديم.
لسنا أخرَ الناجين
ولكن قد ينقذنا عدونا من نفسه
إذا فهم أننا زوج قاتل وقتيل:
وعلينا انتظار بزوغ الأرض في فُلك الدم سَوية.
ربما
لأنه يربي كراهيتنا خلف حواجز لا حاجة له بها.
كم يكرهُنا الحمامُ الذي نسمنه لنأكله

Why Should We Teach Our Enemy How to Raise Pigeons?

Ayman Ghbarieh | Translated by Fady Joudah

Why should we train our enemy how our hands scatter the crumbs?
Why should we insist on showing him how our bread smiles to the beaks?
Why should we teach our enemy how to raise pigeons?
Maybe
because bread is God's name on earth
and the pigeon's memory carries within an ancient flood.
We are not the last survivors
though our enemy might save us from himself
if he understands we are a couple: murderer and murdered
and that we must wait together for the earth to burst out of the orbit of blood.
Maybe
because he nurtures our hate behind checkpoints he has no need of.
O how the pigeons we fatten to eat hate us.

نربيه خارج الأقفاص
ومع ذلك ينتصر حنينه إلى سكاكيننا.
ربما
حين سنعلمه الإنتظار مثلنا
سيتقن استدراجنا
بلا حاجةٍ لاصطيادنا برصاصةٍ من بعيد.
سنقتربُ كالحمام منه بلا وجلٍ
وسيدعنا نسمُن على فضلاتِه.
سيُجبرنا على المشي بدل الطيران
وسيؤسسُ من أجلنا مملكة الدجاج.
ربما
لأننا سنكره عدونا أكثر حين سيشبهنا.
ربما
لأن السخرية أخرَ ما تبقى لنا
قبل أن نترجم كل نكاتنا إلى العبرية.

We don't raise them in cages
yet their longing for our knives triumphs.
Maybe
when we teach him waiting like we wait
he will refine his methods in luring us
without his need for bullets to hunt us from a distance.
We would approach him like pigeons without dread
and he'd let us grow fat on his leftovers.
And force us to walk instead of fly
and establish the Kingdom of Chickens for us.
Maybe
because we'd hate our enemy more when he resembles us.
Maybe
because satire is all that is left to us
before we translate our jokes into Hebrew.

غياب

جالس على مقهى المحطة..
ببدلة كاملة،
وأربعين سنة،
بلا قلق،
بلا أسئلة،
بغير النعاس الذي يرافق المسافرين في المساء.
ربما ينتبه لشارات الوقت البارد
يثرثر مع فراغ كوبه
يهز رأسه كمن يريد أن يقول "لا".
لكنه واثقاً يمضي في جلوسه
والقطارات لا تغادر موعدها،

Absence

Nasser Rabah | Translated by Fady Joudah

sitting in the café at the station

in his suit
and his forty years,
without worry
or questions
and without the sleepiness that accompanies travelers at evening

he might notice the signs of cold time
or chatter with the emptiness of his glass
and shake his head like someone who says

"No"

و المسافرون يحملون ارتباكهم كأمتعة
حنينهم، كمعصية.
ويهربون من كثافة البهاء في المكان.
مرة إلى بوابة القطار،
ومرة إلى بوابة المحطة..
وجالس وحسب،
يومئ للكرسي الخالي في الزاوية الأخرى
من مقهاه..
ببدلة كاملة،
وأربعين سنة..
لا يودع احداً،
لا ينتظر قطاراً ما..
متفهماً تماماً..
لماذا يزينون المحطات بالتماثيل.

but he goes on assured in his sitting
as the trains sit late to their appointments
and the travelers carry their fretfulness like the luggage
of their longing, like sin

and escape from the density of splendor in this place

to the coach door
or to the station's exit

as he simply sits
gesturing to the empty chair in the opposite corner
of his café

in his suit
and his forty years

not saying goodbye to anyone
or waiting for some train

completely aware

why they adorn stations with statues

عُزلة مسيّجة

بيدِكَ المفتاحُ الذي تَحقهُ
أصابعُ تقوّضتْ من الحنين
وأنتَ خلفَ بابٍ أدْمَتهُ طرقاتُ الزّائرين
لا تَخرجْ إلى الهواء السّاهر
لئلا تَمسّكَ أنفاسُ مَن عبروا صدفة
وتَحطمتْ أفواهُهُم مِنَ الصّراخ
الذي حجّرَ النّافذة.

لا تلتفتْ إلى ما يُثمرُ في أشجار العتمةِ
إلى ما يَسقط من لمعان القمر على الحاقة.

أنتَ ما ينعدمُ في جوارِه
كلّ كلامٍ يدورُ على الصّمت
ما لا يَرقى سُلّمٌ إليه
في عُلوِّهِ المُسيّج بأريج أزهار مُهرَّبةٍ
من حدائق غَرقى.
أنتَ ما تَجهلُ كلُّ معرفةٍ خلاصَه.

Fenced Solitude

Ghadah al-Shafi'i | Translated by Sinan Antoon

The key surrounded by fingers
wrecked by longing is in your hand
You are behind a door
bloodied by visitors' knocks
do not go out to the air
lest the breaths of those who pass by coincidence
touch you
those whose mouths have been demolished
by the screaming
which turned the window into stone

do not pay attention to what blooms
in the trees of darkness
to the glittering of the moon
falling on the edges

In your vicinity,
every speech
which revolves around silence
is extinct
You are
what no ladder can climb
in those heights
fenced by the scent of roses
smuggled from drowned gardens
You are one whose salvation
is unknown
to every knowledge

الرجل الجميل جداً

هكذا وَجَدوه
جَسَدٌ ما، وعارٍ فقط
نَبْتَةٌ خَضْراء
كانت تَرْبُطُ ظِلَّهُ بالأرْض
قالتْ:
لكي لا يَسقط في النَوْم سَهْواً
ثمَّ بَكَتْ
هكذا وَجَدوه إذاً
الرَّجُلُ الجميلُ جِدّاً
جَنباً إلى جَنْبٍ
ذاتَ ظهيرةٍ
مع أسْماك.

The Very Handsome Man

Samir Abu Hawwash | Translated by Sinan Antoon

that's how they found him
just a naked body
a green plant
tied his shadow to the earth
she said:
so that he would not fall in his sleep
by mistake
then she wept
so that's how they found him
the very handsome man
one afternoon
side by side
with fish

سرطان

ابنة عمي
صفراء
وصلعاء تماما
كانت تجلس في الصالون
صامتة
وتبتسم للزائرين
انتظروا موتها
تسعة اشهر.

Cancer

Samir Abu Hawwash | Translated by Sinan Antoon

my cousin
pale yellow
totally bald
she was sitting in the guest room
silent
smiling to visitors
who had been waiting nine months
for her death

مريم

أمي مغرمة هذه الأيام بالقراءة عن يسوع، أرى كتباً مكومة قرب سريرها (تستعيرها غالبا من مكتبتي):
روايات وسبل ومذاهب ومؤلفين يتضاربون بالأيدي. ويحدث أن أمراً أحياناً من هناك، فتناديني لكي أحجز
بينهم. (قبل قليل أسعفتُ مؤرخاً يُدعى كمال صليبي وقد شُجّ بحجر كاثوليكي في جبهته!)

ويا لها من قارئة جادة في بحثها عن يسوع، هذه المرأة التي خيّبتُ ظنّها دائما. فلم أستشهد في الانتفاضة
الأولى ولا الثانية ولا الثالثة

كما أني – وهذا بيننا – لن أستشهد في أية انتفاضة قادمة

ولن أقتل في انفجار لقلق ملغوم!

....

....

إنها تقرأ وخيالها الأرثوذكسي يصلبني مع كل صفحة

وأنا لا أفعلُ شيئاً سوى تزويد خيالها بكتب أخرى ومسامير!

Maryam

Najwan Darwish | Translated by Antoine Jockey and Marilyn Hacker

These days, my mother is enthralled in reading about Jesus. I see piles of books near her bed (she often takes them from my own bookshelves): novels, do-it-yourself manuals, books on the sects, quarrelling authors. Sometimes when I'm passing by her bedroom, she calls on me to settle their disputes (not long ago I came to the aid of an Orthodox historian called Kamal Salibi after a Catholic stone had slashed his forehead!)

How serious she is in her research on Jesus, this woman whom I've always disappointed:

I wasn't martyred during the first Intifada, nor during the second, nor even during the third.

Just between us, I'm not going to become a martyr in any Intifada coming up

And I won't die blown up by a booby-trapped stork either!

. . . .

. . . .

She reads, and her Orthodox imagination crucifies me on every page

While all I do is supply her with books and nails!

باص الكوابيس الذاهب إلى صبرا وشاتيلا

رأيتهم يضعون خالاتي في أكياس بلاستيك سوداء
وفي زوايا الأكياس تتجمع دماؤهن الحارة
(لكن أنا ليس لي خالات)
ـعرفت أنهم قد قتلوا ناتاشا ـ ابنتي التي في الثالثة
(لكن أنا ليس لي ابنة)
قيل لي أنهم اغتصبوا زوجتي قبل أن يجرّوا جسمها على الدرج ويتركوه في الشارع
(لكن أنا لم أتزوج)
لا شك هذه نظارتي التي تحطمت تحت البسطار
لكن أنا لا ألبس نظارة!))

....
....

كنتُ نائماً في بيت والديّ أحلم بالسفر إلى بيتها، وحين استيقظت:
رأيت إخوتي

The Nightmare Bus to Sabra and Shatila

Najwan Darwish | Translated by Antoine Jockey and Marilyn Hacker

I saw them stuff my aunts into black plastic sacks
Their hot blood pooled in the corners of the bags
(But I have no aunts)
I knew they had killed Natasha, my three-year-old daughter
(But I have no daughter)
I was told they raped my wife, then dragged her body down the stairs and left it lying in the street
(But I am not married)
Those are certainly my glasses that were crushed under their boots
(But I don't wear glasses)
....
....
I was asleep in my parents' house, dreaming of traveling to her house. When I awoke
I saw my brothers
Hung
From the roof of the Church of the Resurrection

يتدلون
من سقف كنيسة القيامة.
كان الرب يقول من الشفقة: هذا ألمي أنا.
وكنت أستجمع كبرياء المعلقين وأقول: لا بل هذا ألمنا!

....
....

الألم يضيء ويصير أحبّ إليّ من كوابيسي.

....
....

لن أهرب للشمال
أيها الربّ
لا تحسبني من الذين يبحثون عن ملاذ.

سنكمل لاحقاً هذا الحساب ⸺

عليّ أن أمضي الآن إلى النوم:
لا أريد أن أتأخر عن باص الكوابيس، الذاهب إلى صبرا وشاتيلا...

Out of compassion, the Lord said: this is my own suffering.
I mustered up the hanged men's pride and said: in my opinion, it's ours.

....

....

Pain is illuminating , and I have come to love it more than my nightmares.

....

....

I will not flee to the North
Oh Lord
Don't count me among the ones seeking shelter.

....

....

We'll continue this report later.

I've got to go to sleep now.
I don't want to miss the nightmare bus that goes to Sabra and Shatila.

هيَ وهوَ

هيَ..
تعدُّ الصباحَ الأنيقَ
بفنجان قهوةٌ
تمرُّ على حُلْم ليلتها بارتباك:
كأنهُ كان هنا في جواري؟
ترتبُ أيامها في خزانة
و تختارُ يوماً جديداً
بعيداً عن الوقت والتسميات
ففي العمر مُتسعٌ ما يزالُ
لِيوم، بعيداً عن الكلماتْ.

هوَ..
يُفتشُ في خزانتِهِ عن اسم
يليقُ بكلِّ الذي قد يمرُ عليهِ
وقد لا يمُرْ..
يُريدُ اختصاراً لكلِّ الكلام
وكلِّ الحنينْ
وكلِّ الجمالِ
وكلِّ الأنينْ
فلا تعتريهِ سوى الذكرياتْ
وأسماءَ ثكلى

She and He

Hala al-Shrouf | Translated by Wafa'a Abdulaali and Marilyn Hacker

She . . .
Gets ready for a pleasant morning
with strong coffee.
She recalls last night's dream, becomes embarrassed:
and if he were here close to me?
She arranges her days in a closet
chooses a new day
away from time and naming.
In the future there will be many of them,
these days far from words.

He . . .
searches in his own closet for a name
that will fit everything that passes him
and everything that may not.

He wants to be brief in speech
    in nostalgia
    in beauty
    in complaints
So that nothing controls him but memories
orphaned names of his desires.

She . . .
comes back to herself in the evening
with a branch of jasmine
and some fatigue . . .
She brightens her night with a multicolored nightgown
cheats her loneliness with worries
abandons a bed meant for love
to drowse between wishes and insomnia.

هوَ..

يُريدُ لِليلتهِ أن تسيرَ

إلى فجرها مُسرعة

فيُطفئُ كلَّ الشموع

لِتبصرَ عتمتَها في الأفقْ

يُحيكُ تفاصيلهُ من حبقْ.

يضمُّ وسادتَهُ في يديهِ

فيخذلهُ هاجسٌ قد سبقْ.

هيَ..

تعودُ إلى نفسها في المساءْ

بعودٍ من الياسمين

وبعض التعبْ..

تلوّنُ ليلتَها بالقميص المُزركشْ

تغافلُ وحدتَها بالقلقْ

وتتركُ للحبِّ كلَّ السريرْ

لتغفوَ بين الأماني وبين الأرقْ.

He . . .
wants his night to drain away quickly
to dawn
so he snuffs out all the candles
to let them see their darkness on the horizon
goes quickly to his narrow bed
following a seductive dream he is weaving from patches . . .
takes his pillow in his arms
weary of his obsession from the past.

Original Texts

"Rita's Winter" by Mahmoud Darwish. "Shita' Rita" from *Ahad 'ashar kawkaban*. Beirut: Dar al-Jadid, 1992.

"Like One Who Waits for Me" and "He Thought Long of Going Back There" by Ghassan Zaqtan. "Kammen yantatherni" and "Fakker taweelan bil-aoudet hounak" from *Katayir min al-quash yatbaouni*. Beirut: Riyad al-Rayyis lil-Kutub wa-al-Nashr, 2008.

"Why Should We Teach Our Enemies How to Raise Pigeons?" by Ayman Ghbarieh. "Limatha alaina ann nou'allem adouonna tarbiyet al-hamama" from *Le Poème Palestinien Contemporain*, ed. Ghassan Zaqtan. Belgium: Editions Le Taillis Pré, 2008.

"Absence" by Nasser Rabah. "Ghiab" from *Running After a Dead Gazelle*. Ramallah: Palestinian Ministry of Culture, 2003.

"Fenced Solitude" by Ghada al-Shafi'i. "Uzla musayyaja" from *Le Poème Palestinien Contemporain*, ed. Ghassan Zaqtan. Belgium: Editions Le Taillis Pré, 2008.

"The Very Handsome Man" by Samir Abu Hawwash. "Al-rajul al-jamil jiddan" from *al-Hayah tutba' fi Niyu Yurk*. Beirut: Dar al-Jadid, 1997.

"Cancer" by Samir Abu Hawwash. "Saratan" from *Remember, Valentine*. Beirut: Éditions Maintenant, 2002.

"Maryam" and "The Nightmare Bus to Sabra and Shantila" by Najwan Darwish. "Maryam" and "Bas al-kuwabis a-dhahab illa Sabra wa Shatila" from *Le Poème Palestinien Contemporain*, ed. Ghassan Zaqtan. Belgium: Editions Le Taillis Pré, 2008. First published in the London-based newspaper *Al-Quds Al-Arabi* on September 5, 2006.

"She and He" by Hala al-Shrouf. "Hiya wa hua" from *sa'aTba'u ghayman*. Beirut: Dar al-Adab, 2005.

Contributors

Wafa'a Abdulaali teaches English poetry and translation at the University of Mosul. She has been a Fellow of the Radcliffe Institute and a visiting scholar at Harvard Divinity School. Abdulaali co-translated with Sanna Dhahir *Contemporary Poetry From Iraq* by Bushra al-Bustani (Edwin Mellen Press, 2008), and she has a forthcoming collection of fifty modern English poems translated into Arabic.

Kareem James Abu-Zeid is a PhD student in comparative literature at UC Berkeley, focusing on modern Arabic poetry. He has published and presented on translation theory and modern Arabic literature. He is the translator of the Sudanese novel *Cities Without Palms* by Tarek Eltayeb (American University of Cairo Press, 2009).

Esther Allen is an assistant professor at Baruch College, CUNY. Her previous translations that are most closely related to her work with José Manuel Prieto are the Penguin Classics anthology *José Martí: Selected Writings*, which she also edited and annotated, and *Selected Non-Fictions* by Jorge Luis Borges (Viking, 1999), which she co-translated with Eliot Weinberger and Suzanne Jill Levine. In 2009–2010 she will be a Fellow at the Cullman Center for Scholars and Writers in the New York Public

Library, working on an edited and annotated translation of Adolfo Bioy Casares's *Borges*, a portrait of Borges through a half-century's worth of diary entries kept by his best friend and literary collaborator.

Alison Anderson is a novelist and translator of J.M.G. Le Clézio, Muriel Barbery, Amélie Nothomb, and Anna Gavalda, among others. She presently resides in a small village in Switzerland. Other work by Christian Bobin will be published in her translation by Autumn Hill Books in 2009.

Sinan Antoon's poems and essays have appeared in *Ploughshares, World Literature Today, BOMB,* and *The Nation.* He is the author of *The Baghdad Blues* (Harbor Mountain Press, 2007) and *I'jaam: An Iraqi Rhapsody* (City Lights, 2007). His translation of Mahmoud Darwish's *The Presence of Absence* is forthcoming from Archipelago Books.

Elizabeth Bell is a San Francisco-based translator whose recent work appears in *Island of My Hunger: Cuban Poetry Today* (City Lights, 2007) and *The Best of Contemporary Mexican Fiction* (Dalkey Archive Press, 2009). Translation fulfills two of her childhood dreams: to mate with language and to disappear.

Susan Bernofsky is the translator of four books by the Swiss-German modernist author Robert Walser as well as novels by Jenny Erpenbeck, Yoko Tawada, Hermann Hesse, Gregor von Rezzori, and others. She is currently working on a biography of Walser and writing a novel set in her hometown of New Orleans.

Karen Emmerich's translations include *I'd Like* (Dalkey Archive Press, 2008) by Amanda Michalopoulou, and *Poems (1945-1971)* (Archipelago Books, 2006) by Miltos Sachtouris. She is the recipient of grants and awards from the NEA, PEN, and the Modern Greek Studies Association.

Edward Gauvin has been an ALTA fellow and a resident at the Ledig House and the Banff International Translation Centre. His translation of Georges-Olivier

Châteaureynaud's *A Life on Paper: Selected Stories* is forthcoming from Small Beer Press. Other translations have appeared in *AGNI*, *Conjunctions*, *Words Without Borders*, *Epiphany*, *Absinthe*, *Fantasy & Science Fiction*, and *The Brooklyn Rail*.

Choman Hardi was born in Kurdistan and raised in Iraq and Iran. She studied at Queens College, Oxford, University College London, and the University of Kent at Canterbury. She has published three collections of poetry in Kurdish. Her first English collection is *Life for Us* (Bloodaxe Books, 2004).

Ellen Hinsey is the author of *Update on the Descent* (Bloodaxe Books, 2009), *The White Fire of Time* (Wesleyan University Press, 2002), and *Cities of Memory*, which received the Yale Younger Poets Award (1995). Her work has appeared in the *New York Times*, the *New Yorker,* and the *Paris Review*. Also a translator from French, she has received a Lannan Foundation Award and a Berlin Prize Fellowship from the American Academy. She lives in Paris.

A Wyoming native, **Jon Jensen** holds degrees in Russian, classics, and rhetoric. He studied at the Russian Academy of Sciences and served in the Peace Corps in Moscow. Jensen teaches at the Kingsborough English Language Institute and studies poetry at City College of New York. His poems are forthcoming in *J Journal*.

Antoine Jockey was born in Beirut in 1966 and now lives in Paris. He has translated many Arabic-language poets into French, including Abbas Beydoun, Sargon Boulus, Abdelkader al-Jannabi, and Joumana Haddad. His translation of an anthology of new Palestinian poetry, *La poeme palestinien*, was published by Le Taillis Pré in 2008.

Fady Joudah is the author of *The Earth in the Attic*, which received the Yale Younger Poets Award in 2007. He was awarded the 2008 Saif Ghobash-Banipal Prize for Arabic Literary Translation for his translation of Mahmoud Darwish's *The Butterfly's Burden* (Copper Canyon Press, 2006). His newest volume of translations of Darwish, *If I Were Another,* is forthcoming from Farrar, Straus & Giroux. Joudah is a physician and field member with Doctors Without Borders.

J. Kates is a poet and literary translator who lives in Fitzwilliam, New Hampshire.

Rika Lesser's latest books are *Questions of Love: New & Selected Poems* (Sheep Meadow Press, 2008) and a retranslation of Hesse's *Siddhartha: An Indic Poem* (Barnes & Noble Classics, 2007). She is the recipient of the Harold Morton Landon Translation Prize of the Academy of American Poets for Gunnar Ekelöf's *Guide to the Underworld* (1982) and the American-Scandinavian Foundation Translation Prize (2002).

Elizabeth Macklin is the author of *A Woman Kneeling in the Big City* (W. W. Norton, 1994) and *You've Just Been Told* (W. W. Norton, 2000). An Amy Lowell Scholarship in 1999 led to her translate Kirmen Uribe's *Meanwhile*

Take My Hand (Graywolf Press, 2007), a finalist for the 2008 PEN Translation Fund Award. She is working on a third collection and the translation of *Bilbao–New York–Bilbao.*

Khaled Mattawa is the author of *Zodiac of Echoes* (Ausable Press, 2003), *Ismailia Eclipse* (Sheep Meadow Press, 1995), and *Amorisco* (Ausable Press, 2008), and he has co-edited two anthologies of Arab-American literature. Mattawa has translated seven volumes of contemporary Arabic poetry by Saadi Youssef, Fadhil al-Azzawi, Hatif al-Janabi, Maram al-Massri, Iman Mersal, and Joumana Haddad. He teaches at the University of Michigan, Ann Arbor.

Chris Michalski's work has appeared in *Poetry International*, *Puerto del Sol*, *The Marlboro Review*, and *Spoon River Poetry Review*. He is the author of *paper route and other poems* (littlefishcart press, 2007). His manuscript of selected poems and texts by Stanislaw Borokowski, "waiting to go under," is seeking publication.

Breon Mitchell is a professor of Germanic studies and comparative literature and director of the Lilly Library at Indiana University, and a past president of the American Literary Translators Association. He was awarded the Kurt and Helen Wolff Prize for his translation of Uwe Timm's *Morenga* in 2004.

Denise Newman is the translator of Inger Christensen's *The Painted Room* (Harvill Press, 2000) and the author of two poetry collections, *Human Forest* (2000) and *Wild Goods* (2008), both from Apogee Press. Her work has appeared in *ZYZZYVA*, *Denver Quarterly*, *Volt*, and *Terrestrial Intelligence*. She teaches at the California College of the Arts in San Francisco.

Rasheeda Plenty is pursuing an MFA in poetry at the University of Michigan. She is currently working on a poetry manuscript and a translation of Ibrahim Nasrallah's *In the Name of the Mother and the Son*.

Anita Sagástegui is a native speaker of both English and Spanish. She is a Spanish and French literary translator, and also teaches translation and poetry to grade school children in the Poetry Inside Out program. One of her most recent translations appears in *Best of Contemporary Mexican Fiction* (Dalkey Archive Press, 2009).

Donna Stonecipher is the author of three books of poetry: *The Reservoir* (University of Georgia Press, 2002), *Souvenir de Constantinople* (Instance Press, 2007), and *The Cosmopolitan* (Coffee House Press, 2008), which won the 2007 National Poetry Series, selected by John Yau. She translates poetry and prose from French and German.

Yerra Sugarman is the author of *The Bag of Broken Glass* (2008) and *Forms of Gone* (2002), both from Sheep Meadow Press. *Forms of Gone* received the PEN/Joyce Osterweil Poetry Award. She has also received a "Discovery"/The Nation Prize, a Bogin Award, a Hemley Award, a Glenna Luschei *Prairie Schooner* Award, and a Canada Council Grant. She teaches at Rutgers University.

George Szirtes's thirteen books of poetry in English include *The Slant Door* (Secker and Warburg, 1979), winner of the Faber Prize, *Reel* (Bloodaxe Books, 2004), winner of the T. S. Eliot Prize, and *New and Collected Poems* (Bloodaxe Books, 2008). He has won many prizes as a translator of poetry and fiction from the Hungarian.

Willard Wood has recently translated an eco-thriller by Jean-Christophe Rufin, *The Scent of Adam* (Lakeshore Entertainment/TF1), and an imagined autobiography of the French Romantic poet Marceline Desbordes-Valmore, tentatively titled *Only To Go* by Anne Plantagenet (Other Press, 2010). He is the recipient of a PEN Translation Fund grant. He lives and works in Norfolk, Connecticut.

Editors

Lauded for her translations of Nobel Laureate José Saramago's novels of the last decade, including *Seeing*, **Margaret Jull Costa** has also brought the work of Fernando Pessoa into English, for which she received the Portuguese Translation Prize. Costa also translates from Spanish, her work with novelist Javier Marías having garnered an International IMPAC Dublin Literary Award and the Premio Valle-Inclán for Spanish Translation. Most recently, she was awarded both the PEN Translation Prize and the Oxford Weidenfeld Translation Prize for her translation of *The Maias* by Eça de Queiroz. Costa's latest translation is *The Accordionist's Son* by Basque novelist Bernardo Atxaga.

Distinguished with the first ever Robert Fagles Translation Prize, **Marilyn Hacker** has published numerous volumes of her translations of poets Vénus Khoury-Ghata, Claire Malroux, Emmanuel Moses, and Guy Goffette. She was awarded the 2009 PEN Award for Poetry in Translation for Marie Étienne's *King of a Hundred Horsemen*. Also the author of twelve books of poetry, most recently *Essays on Departure* and *Desesperanto*, Hacker has been a recipient of the National Book Award, two Lambda Literary Awards, the Lenore Marshall Poetry Prize, and an Award in Literature from the American Academy of Arts and Letters. This year she was appointed a Chancellor of the Academy of American Poets.

Index

by author

Index

by Title

Index

by Language

A Note on the Translations

Original texts appear across from their translations. Where feasible, the entire original text is provided for each of the translations; however, space concerns have prevented the inclusion of more than the first page of prose pieces. Excerpts are marked by spaced ellipses. Copyright permission remains the responsibility of the contributors.

In order to express regional differences in language usage, we make every attempt to locate the authors within the literary tradition of a particular country or geographical region. The region is indicated in parentheses following the language on each title page.

In selections by British translators, British spellings and language use are retained. However, punctuation may be changed to conform to TWO LINES styles.

Acknowledgments

Pp. 18–26 excerpted from *The Tin Drum* by Günter Grass. Copyright © 1959 by Hermann Luchterhand Verlag GmbH. Translation copyright © 2009 by Breon Mitchell. Reprinted by permission of Houghton Mifflin Harcourt Publishing Company. All rights reserved.

Pp. 38–44 excerpted from *Rex* by José Manuel Prieto. Copyright © 2003 by José Manuel Prieto. Translation copyright © 2009 by Esther Allen. Used by permission of Grove/Atlantic, Inc.

Pp. 106–117 excerpted from *The Naked Eye* by Yoko Tawada. Copyright © 2004 by Yoko Tawada and Konkursbuch Verlag Claudia Gehrke. Translation copyright © Susan Bernofsky. Used by permission of New Directions Publishing Corporation.

Pp. 130–140 excerpted from *Azorno* by Inger Christensen. Copyright © 1967 by Inger Christensen and Gyldendal. Translation copyright © by Denise Newman. Used by permission of New Directions Publishing Corporation.

Pp. 154–162 excerpted from *Cities Without Palms* by Tarek Eltayeb. Copyright © 1992 Tarek Eltayeb. Translation copyright © by Kareem James Abu-Zeid. Used by permission of the American University in Cairo Press.

Sincere thanks to Keith Ekiss, Anne Posten, Elisabeth Friedeman, Maria Gould, Kareem Abu-Zeid, and Tag Savage for their work on this project.

About TWO LINES

For sixteen years, TWO LINES has published translations of poetry and fiction from more than fifty languages and fifty countries. Every edition features the best in international writing, showcasing diverse new writing alongside the world's most celebrated literature and presenting exclusive insight from translators into the creative art of translation. Through the annual volume of TWO LINES World Writing in Translation and the World Library, TWO LINES opens the borders of world literature to give readers access to the most vibrant writing from around the world.

TWO LINES is a program of the Center for the Art of Translation, a non-profit organization that promotes international literature and translation through the arts, education, and community outreach. The Center aims to make global voices and great literature accessible to readers and communities through the TWO LINES publications; the Poetry Inside Out educational program, and Lit&Lunch, the only bilingual reading series spotlighting translation. The Center was created to bring readers and writers together across borders and languages. Through each of its programs, the Center promotes translation and world writing as a vital bridge not just between languages, but between people.

Order copies of TWO LINES or find out more about the Center at www.catranslation.org.

في حديثها عن حقلهما

Ibrahim Nasrallah

التينُ والزيتونُ
والسروُ الدوالي
المرْيَميّةُ في ظلال البرتقال
وريحةُ الليمون
فوحُ الياسمينةِ في الليالي
اللوزهُ الخضراءُ
والرمانةُ العنّابُ
والمشمشُ والصّبيرُ
صفصاف المواجع في الأعالي
الحَوَرُ والريحانُ
.. روحُك
والبدنْ
ها كلُّ شيء ههنا في حقل منفانا تماماً
مثلما في أرضنا الأولى..
ولم يَدُر الزمنْ
لنَحُسَّ نصفَ دقيقةٍ
أنَّ المنافي كالوطنْ

She Talks About Their Field

Translated by Rasheeda Plenty from Arabic (Palestine)

The fig and the olive
and the trellis evergreen cypress,
the sage in the shelter of oranges
and the scent of lemon,
the fragrance of jasmine in the night,
the green almond,
of the jujube pomegranate,
the apricot and Indian fig,
the aching willow on the heights,
the white poplar and sweet basil
. . . your soul
and the body.
Look there. Everything is here in the field of our exile
like in our first earth
and time did not turn us
to feel for half a minute
that exile is like home.